C0053 91534

KT-443-032

**Parkhead Library**
Tollcross Road
G31 4XA

Fax 276 1531

L

C
n

# Shadow Shooters

Released from Yuma Prison in the fall of 1878, after serving three years for bank robbery, Anson Hawkstone returns to the Apache village where he lived, determined to find Rachel, his former love, and give up the outlaw trail. However, things do not go as planned when he is forced to take part in a stage-coach hold-up after Hattie, an Apache princess, is taken hostage. Hawkstone is pushed to the limit in trying to avenge the wrongs committed by other men before he can finally be reunited with Rachel.

*By the same author writing as George Snyder*

The Gunman and the Angel
Dry Gulch Outlaws

# Shadow Shooters

George Arthur

A Black Horse Western

ROBERT HALE

© George Arthur 2018
First published in Great Britain 2018


ISBN 978-0-7198-2659-7


The Crowood Press
The Stable Block
Crowood Lane
Ramsbury
Marlborough
Wiltshire SN8 2HR

www.bhwesterns.com

Robert Hale is an imprint
of The Crowood Press

The right of George Arthur to be identified as
author of this work has been asserted by him
in accordance with the Copyright, Designs and
Patents Act 1988

All rights reserved. No part of this publication may be
reproduced or transmitted in any form or by any means,
electronic or mechanical, including photocopying, recording,
or any information storage and retrieval system, without
permission in writing from the publishers.

Typeset by
Derek Doyle & Associates, Shaw Heath
Printed and bound in Great Britain by
CPI Group (UK) Ltd, Croydon, CR0 4YY

# ONE

They released him the second week of August, 1878. He stepped out of Yuma Territorial Prison into the harsh, gritty Arizona wind carrying a bundle under his arm, his tousled, curly blond hair whipping round his face in the breeze; he wore plain blue denim pants, a white shirt buttoned at the wrists and neck, and high-topped shoes. His hazel eyes squinted at the waiting buckboard.

The old Apache woman stood next to the wheel, crouched against the wind, her craggy face weathered as river driftwood. She held the grey plains Stetson hat in both hands while she watched him approach.

'You need haircut, Anson Hawkstone,' the old woman said, handing him the Stetson.

They stood close, facing each other, he towering above her at his six feet four. The old woman looked ancient and creased from the 200-mile trip out.

Hawkstone pulled the Stetson on to his head. 'Where is the woman, Big Ears Kate?'

'She is with the man.'

'The same man?'

'Pine Oliver he calls himself, the man in your house, on your bed, inside Big Ears Kate.'

'Didn't visit once in three years,' Hawkstone said. 'You

5

came every month, 400 miles round about.'

The old woman shook against a gust of hot wind, looking weary, her frail frame light enough to blow away. 'Some brand woman can't wait three years – too long to pine – gets restless with yearning and want – finds substitutes.'

Hawkstone helped her up to the buckboard seat. She took the reins.

'I'll drive,' he said. 'Slide over.'

The old Apache woman in her loose buckskin did not move. 'Free from prison you take command?'

'I command nothing, but I'll drive the wagon. Slide over.'

She slid away, but held the reins. He climbed to the seat beside her and tossed the bundle in the back. He smiled at her, content to see her without bars between them, and pulled the reins from her hands. 'You raised me from a pup, and mebbe even past forty don't make me no good.'

'You still pup in some ways.' Her eyes looked ahead, her face sharp, durable as stone without expression, without softness. She placed her creased hand on his leg.

Hawkstone waved the reins against the back of the mule.

With darkness they camped along the Rio Gila, to split the trip into four days. They ate smoked antelope she had brought. She slept inside the wagon without movement, while Hawkstone tossed restless on the ground under the wagon, listening to the gurgle of the Rio Gila and coyotes on the prowl.

The village of twenty tepees and four wickiups looked the same to him, clustered close along a flat between hills approaching the Pinon Llano mountains. Juniper and mesquite clung to the craggy hillsides, with cottonwood along the creeks and the big Rio Gila river. The village was forty miles north of Fort Grant and Wharton City, Arizona

Territory, a day's ride south of Tucson. A mile from the village was the house that he had built – the house where Big Ears Kate shared his bed with a man called Pine Oliver.

Inside the old woman's wickiup where as a child he had grown up, he dropped the bundle and pawed through his gear from a life before prison – his buckskin pants, three cotton shirts, boots and his gunbelt.

The old woman watched the bundle unroll. 'You still carry book.'

Hawkstone picked up the thin volume. 'Ben Franklin.'

'He come to village?'

'He's long dead. He wrote words I read and say sometimes, as I remember.'

She nodded. 'You go to house now?'

'It ain't moving. I'll be getting to it.' He picked up the 1876 Winchester rifle. He held the Colt Peacemaker .45 in his hand. 'Where's my Mexican saddle?'

'On Black Feather's pinto – a good saddle should not be idle.'

'It won't be idle now I'm back.'

'He will bring it.'

The old woman sat cross-legged Apache fashion and watched Hawkstone.

He said, 'I'm headed to Disappointment Creek – wash this prison stench off me.'

'I will cook venison before dark.' She stared at him. 'Big Ears Kate will push her parts against you so you smile on her.'

'*Tricks and treachery are the practice of fools without wit enough to be honest.*'

The old woman nodded. 'Is that from the book?'

'It is, sort of.'

She said, 'Will you know when false words of honey come from her?'

7

'*Monkeys full of spite will always come round to bite.*' He winked at the old woman as he carried his clothes from the wickiup down towards the creek.

Village dogs not knowing him yapped out a barking chorus, tails wagging friendly while he talked low to them as he walked and told them they were good puppies. He carried the bundle fifty yards from the village to the creek and dropped it on the bank. Two young girls hauled their clean laundry away with giggles. When they were out of sight, he tore the prison-issued clothes off his body until he was naked – ripped the buttons off the shirt, yanked the pants down his legs, and threw it all in the creek, so the clothes and the memory of where they came from washed down to the big Rio Gila river and drowned.

He sat in the stream flow and splashed water over his chest and waist and head. The creek was cold, but felt good in the heat of the setting sun. He stretched his back out on smooth rocks until the water flowed over his head. He moved his head from side to side while he scrubbed himself all over with his bare hands. With his head propped on a slick pile of pebbles, he watched scarlet clouds move slowly above him.

He brought into his mind an image of Big Ears Kate. When he thought of her it was only her soft body he remembered – much softness – excess softness. Her face was smooth and quick to smile, with fleshy lips that she opened easily – apparently for anyone.

By contrast there had been the woman in prison, Pearl Harp – the only woman ever inside, a stagecoach robber whom Hawkstone knew intimately for almost a year. Pearl was a tiny thing, no more than five feet two and slight. Her interesting face could be attractive when she worked at it, otherwise she looked downright masculine. Past thirty yet firm as a young tree trunk, she wasn't eager about anything except making her way through prison time as easy as she could. Hawkstone had met her his second year in, and their intimacy didn't go quite a year: the warden had taken a liking to her, and he was able to make her life much easier than Hawkstone could. He snatched her right away. Her company kept the warden smiling, until she became in the family way.

The child was picked up by her well-off parents from Illinois, and joined the other two they raised by her divorced husband, Brett Harp. After the divorce, Pearl had worked a few tents while travelling the country, and had then hooked up with an outlaw, Boot Hobson, and taken to stagecoach holdups. They never made much money at it, mostly what the passengers carried. Boot had cut a trail to parts unknown, and Pearl went to prison for stealing $436. The warden had made promises for early release, and had actually been working on it while he worked on her.

The sun had almost hidden behind the Pinons. Hawkstone felt the bubble of the creek water wash over him. Parts of prison needed time to fade. Ben Franklin wrote that time was a herb that cured all diseases, or something like that. Prison life would fade because he intended to replace it with better parts of living.

Thinking of Big Ears Kate and Pearl Harp just naturally had him calling to mind Rachel Cleary, who later became Rachel Good Squaw. She had crowded his thoughts in prison, as she had at sea. Sometimes she pushed out the sounds of imprisoned men with their shouts, their cries and tears, vomiting and fighting each other. So many years ago, before the events of his life swept him along. He was eighteen, she was sixteen, and they had been in love.

# TWO

The splash of the creek made Anson Hawkstone doze and remember. When he was ten, his parents had been killed and he had been taken by Cherokee; but he had run off, and these Chiricahua Apache had found him starving in the desert, and the old woman – younger then, with a son and his new woman – had taken him to raise until grandchildren came along. When Hawkstone reached seventeen, the son's squaw had given the old woman a baby granddaughter – but Hawkstone then left for the goldfields of California.

A year later he had met the orphan Irish girl with flaming red hair and an easy laugh named Rachel Cleary – except, at eighteen, a chance had come to Hawkstone that he couldn't let go: he hired on as a deck hand for the clipper ship *Roberta Cloud*, bound round the world hauling cargo of all kinds. Hawkstone's thinking was that he might find his Norwegian roots and where his people came from – or if he still had people. He wrestled with the decision to go – but he couldn't afford to take her with him.

He didn't know he had left Rachel in the family way.

Over the next seven years, Anson Hawkstone rose to captain his own clipper, the *Rose Wave*, which sailed him to meet relatives in Norway and to other ports of the world. Though many women passed through his bunk and life, his fondness remained for the Irish girl, Rachel Cleary. He wrote to her when he could, but his letters came back. In 1858, at twenty-five, he left the sea, having found the history

10

of his roots, and after experiencing many other worldly adventures. After a year of failed searching to find Rachel, he settled in Santa Fe, New Mexico Territory, where he met and married a pretty, sweet girl named Susan who gave him his baby boy, Michael. He began to scout for the army.

A year later he was dispatched to Fort McDowell, east of Wickenburg in Arizona Territory. He joined a cavalry expedition of forty soldiers riding southwest, where a tribe of Mescalero Apache had been reported running kill raids against the locals outside the town of Globe. Hawkstone took no part in the killing, having been raised by Apache and with no animosity towards them. He showed the army the way, then avoided the massacre – and suppressed his urge to open fire on the blue bellies by riding off. Then his attention was caught by a pinto running fast across the mesa, a woman bent over its neck, wounded. Her bright red hair flowed like a banner behind her. Hawkstone rode after her, rode her down until he could halt the pinto. He pulled her off the horse and carried her into an old mining cave.

'Rachel?' he said.

She stared at him with hard green Irish eyes, her face red with riding and the wounds and the country.

She pulled a knife and tried to stab him: 'Kill you,' she said.

Because she was weak from loss of blood, he easily took the knife away. Then she blacked out, which allowed him to dress the wounds in her shoulder and arm. He stared at her while she slept at the entrance to the shallow cave. Below her bottom lip a vertical tattoo line ran straight to the end of her chin. She wore a buckskin dress to her knees with calf-length moccasins. Except for her hair and skin, she looked as Apache as a native woman.

But it was the same Rachel he had known in California all those years before. But she was a captive white woman

11

living with the Apache, and he was married with a baby boy, and scouted for the army. But she had been the first white woman for him – the first love that no man ever forgot.

She woke and they talked. He hadn't known about the child. It had been a girl, still-born. In tears she told him she had named the girl Peggy. The Christian orphanage kicked Rachel out for being of low morals. As Hawkstone listened he felt the heavy weight of responsibility. She had been on a stagecoach headed for Kansas City to business school, when a Cherokee raiding party jumped the stage – Rachel and three other girls were taken captive. One of the girls killed herself with a stolen pistol; Rachel and the two remaining girls were marched south, and traded for horses with the Apache. The brave, strong warriors rode their ponies while the hungry, thirsty girls marched. When they reached Apache territory, she never saw the other girls again. Years went by and she accepted her life.

A brave took her as his own. She soon had a son, and raised him to be a warrior. The brave did not beat her often, and treated her as well as another man might. But in a skirmish with soldiers, the brave and the son were killed. The tribe had changed her name to Rachel Good Squaw, and other Apache suitors pushed for her favour, for she was attractive in an unusual way with that red hair, and had earned a reputation as a good, dutiful woman who usually obeyed her man. But she chose nobody. She had her own sod lean-to built by the men who wanted her. It was on a rise about a quarter mile from the village. She grew a garden. Some of the vegetables she traded for deer and antelope meat. Men offered her horses and goods if she would choose them. But she chose none of them, and she gave herself to no one.

At twenty-seven, Rachel Good Squaw was hardened to her life. In the cave she told Hawkstone she felt little

12

heartache over village people slaughtered by soldiers. She lived with the Apache, but did not love them. She had a few friends, but nobody close. She had thought of returning to the white world, but no man would have her now: she was tainted and branded, and she reckoned it was too late for a life living among Christians of judgment. She needed no man, and had become comfortable living alone.

Hawkstone felt traces of the same affection return as he listened to her, though she was not the same girl he had left. He told her he had thought of her often while he sailed the world. He told her that when he had left the sea he married because he could not find her. She asked if he loved his wife. He said he might have. Susan was a loving wife who worshipped him with more open honesty than anyone ever had. He saw softness return to Rachel's hard green eyes. But she wondered, if he truly loved his wife, how could he leave her to scout for the army? She told him she would have nothing to do with him while he was married.

There was no future for them.

In Disappointment Creek, the stream of water had turned too cold, and Hawkstone pushed himself out of the flow. He dressed as sunset clothed the mountains around him.

On a rise across the creek he saw Hattie Smooth Water standing with her arms out. 'Anson Hawkstone has returned!' she shouted. 'He will claim what is his! Five horses, Anson Hawkstone!' She slid the buckskin dress over her head, wearing only the calf-moccasins. She turned slowly, arms out, to show off her naked, twenty-year-old perfect body. 'Yours for only five horses, Anson!'

Her vicious wolf-dog, Volcano, growled at him as the princess danced, her waist-length black hair bouncing around her bare shoulders.

\*

13

A chestnut mare wearing the Mexican saddle waited at the old woman's wickiup. A small stick and mesquite fire crackled in front of the entrance. The old woman handed a warm piece of venison from the fire to Hawkstone. Black Feather squatted in front of the standing chestnut, the reins in his left hand, venison in his right.

Other men walked by and nodded greetings. The village air was clouded with smoke from small greenwood fires.

'Welcome home, my blood brother,' Black Feather said. He held the reins up to him. 'A returning gift.'

Black Feather moved with the grace of youth – twenty-three, straight black hair to his shoulders, buckskin-dressed, six feet and handsome, a Colt .45 on his hip – many maidens and non-maidens wanted him. On occasion he would choose one for temporary company. He could track a snake across a mountain range of smooth boulders.

The old woman said, 'I go to my bed now.' She touched Black Feather on the shoulder, then Hawkstone on the chest, and ducked into the wickiup.

The venison finished, Hawkstone squatted beside his blood brother. 'You have your own place?'

'A tepee the other side of the village, easy to move – sometimes my sister shares it.'

'Your sister danced naked for me at the creek.'

'She is a foolish girl. Leave her to young bucks easily impressed. Burning Buffalo wants her. You will turn your old eyes away.'

'Hard to do when she dances like that.'

'You do not have five horses or a wedding bed for her.'

'There is the house.'

'And are there the horses?'

'Perhaps the old woman might take fewer than five.'

'Hattie is a Chiricahua princess. Burning Buffalo will

offer more.'

'I might buy horses with the stolen money.'

Black Feather squinted at him. 'Others will come looking for that money. You think they forget in three years?'

'Has anyone been around?'

'Marshal Leather Yates – twice – wanted to know if you come here when you get out, and exactly when you get out.'

Hawkstone rubbed his jowls. 'Yates,' he said.

'You know, he is the marshal at Wharton City.'

'Why would he care?'

'You better take the money and ride out. Keep riding.'

'I don't want to leave Saguaro Claw just yet.'

'The old woman is used to your wanderings – and the outlaw trail you ride. I will go with you if you wish.'

'Somebody has to look after her.'

Black Feather nodded. They rested in silence for a spell, looking down at the ground. 'I put fire water in the saddle-bag,' he said, talking silly Indian as a joke.

'That is a bad place.'

Black Feather stood and pulled the bottle. He opened it and handed it to Hawkstone. He squatted again beside his blood brother and took his turn when offered. 'What you do now?'

Hawkstone said, 'Tomorrow, I deal with the house.'

'You want another gun?'

'I understand there's just the one man – and Big Ears Kate.'

'You may not want to shoot anyone with a marshal sneaking around.'

'If a marshal comes poking into something that ain't none of his business – maybe I'll shoot him, too.'

# THREE

On the floor of the wickiup with his wool blanket, Hawkstone listened to the soft sigh of the sleeping old woman. He tried to keep his tossing quiet.

Hawkstone's thinking went back to Rachel Cleary – Rachel Good Squaw, who in that cave so many years ago, had told him there was no future for them because he was married. For a brief moment he had thought about sending his young wife Susan and his son Michael back to her parents. He had married her because he couldn't find his Rachel. But Susan was a loving and worshipping woman – no man would find a better wife. He had immediately dismissed the thought of leaving her, and hated himself for even thinking it. He had then accepted there was no longer any future with Rachel.

He had left Rachel in the cave with her pinto nearby, and rejoined the cavalry.

When he returned to Santa Fe, he learned that Susan and his son Michael were no more. A week before they had been in a bank when it was robbed, and a dynamite explosion to blow the safe had torn mother and son and two others beyond recognition. He had stared at the shredded remains, recognizing blonde woman curls and the jagged remnants of a boy's small foot, while the marshal touched his shoulder and talked low with sympathy. Because of what he had been thinking about his wife and son, he hated himself enough to go to pieces – emotion and human morality sucked out of his chest, leaving it hollow, with

16

nothing inside him but empty hatred, much aimed at himself. He didn't ask the marshal about his lost family – he asked about the robbers.

In the time it took to find the killers, Anson Hawkstone turned no good.

He found and gunned down the four bank robbers without mercy. He stampeded along the outlaw trail, killing others good and bad. Eventually back with the old woman and Apaches, the year became 1863, and there was a war on. Texas and New Mexico Territory had gone with the Confederacy, and it looked as if Arizona Territory would do the same. Some Fort soldiers went north for new duties fighting against the Johnny Rebs, and Hawkstone reckoned he might as well kill for some cause he didn't care about – so he joined the grey coats, and his life became more blood and gunsmoke.

There truly was no possible future with Rachel Good Squaw.

*The sleeping fox catches no poultry.*

An hour before dawn, Hawkstone left the old woman's wickiup and rode towards his house, letting the chestnut slowly pick her way in the dark. Halfway there he heard Black Feather ride his pinto up behind.

'I think you need another gun,' he said.

'Why?'

'You are digging up the money, right?'

'I am. A shovel is hidden in the pine growth.'

'There is much guessing over the amount.'

'Guessing by who?'

'By me and the old woman – and likely others we can only reckon.'

'It is ten thousand dollars.'

Black Feather sat tall. 'Is that it? I was only twenty, but the bank said you robbers took fifty thousand.'

'The bank lied. It was half that, and Federal Marshal Casey Steel grabbed fifteen thousand after my so-called fellow bandits turned me in.'

'Still, that might be enough to kill a man for.'

'I did three years for it.'

'You think that makes it yours?'

'When I have it in my saddle-bag it will be mine.'

They rode in silence through fading darkness. When Hawkstone saw the dark shadow of his lean-to one-bedroom shack, he turned the chestnut to the left to skirt round the back. Twenty yards beyond began the strand of pines. He circled so the pines stood between him and the house. Black Feather followed. Back beyond the pines, they dismounted. Hawkstone located the rusty shovel. With Black Feather watching, he paced off fifty steps to an open trench and started to dig. Two feet down the shovel hit the canvas bank bag with worm holes. Hawkstone pulled it up and opened it. Cut-up newspaper from three years ago showed inside. He set the bag on the ground. Under the bag was a tin box. When he opened the lid a wood box showed inside. He opened that, and fingered the cash.

A man coughed in the house. He grumbled something.

A woman murmured in a voice thick with sleep, 'I don't hear nothin'.'

Lantern light flickered through pine trunks from the back window. Chairs scraped. The man coughed again. 'I tell ya, somebody is out there.'

'Nothin' is out there,' the woman said. 'Come back to bed. I got this itch.'

'Don't he get out soon?'

'He won't come here. You're too mean for him.'

'It's his house. He'll be comin' for the money. I swear he's got it hidden somewhere in here. Mebbe *he'll* want to take care of your itch.'

'Nobody does that good as you. Come on. Leave the lantern lit. Here, have yourself a good look.'

'Damn,' he said.

'You like what you see? Come here to mama. Get yourself in this bed.'

Grunts came from the house.

Hawkstone left the open hole unfilled, leaving the empty, wormy bank canvas bag. He carried the metal box and the money-stuffed wooden box to the mare, and shoved them in saddle-bags. He nodded away from the pines and mounted. Black Feather threw his leg on to his pinto.

A high, long scream came from the house. 'Oh, Pine, you're the best,' the woman cried.

'Better'n him?' the man asked.

'Oh, way better.' She screamed again.

Hawkstone eased the chestnut away, while Black Feather chuckled.

'That will be Big Ears Kate doing what she does best – lying,' Hawkstone said as they rode off.

Sunrise greeted them back at the old woman's wickiup. She had scrambled eggs and antelope strips in a pan over the campfire. The girl, Hattie Smooth Water, helped her spread wooden plates and stolen silver spoons on logs around the fire. Beyond the space humans gathered, while the half-wild wolf-dog, Volcano, lay staring, his gaze seldom leaving the princess maiden.

Hawkstone watched the old woman move slowly – a great-grandmother she had to be, crawling towards ninety. By contrast, Hattie moved, sitting and standing, with the lithe smoothness of dance steps. She watched Hawkstone tie the chestnut to a juniper. When he turned, she threw her arms around his neck and clung to him.

'You are back to me, Anson. I am not a girl of sixteen any longer, I am a grown woman.'

Hawkstone stepped away from her. 'Almost,' he said. 'But can you cook?'

Even the old woman allowed a slight smile.

Hattie Smooth Water, the Chiricahua princess, indeed made Anson Hawkstone think of her as a woman – at least physically. The top of her head came to his chin. Her frame was long and willowy because of her youth, and her skin showed the smoothness of polished redwood. Her straight, shining black hair hung straight to her buckskin-covered waist. Dark, smoky, sultry, almond-shaped Apache eyes locked on his face and never left, with a bold, open, honest expectance.

Food was dropped on their wooden plates, and they sat on logs to eat.

Hattie said, 'Now you will buy the horses so we can join together.'

Hawkstone smiled at her. 'I'm thinking maybe I'm too young to marry.'

She used her thumb to push her hair behind her ear. 'There will only be you, Anson, and I have waited long enough.'

Black Feather said, 'You talk foolishness, little girl.'

The old woman looked up at Hawkstone. 'You tell a Ben Franklin now.'

Hawkstone said, '*Twenty is the age of will, thirty the age of wit, forty the age of judgment.*'

# FOUR

Wharton City Marshal Leather Yates rode out to the Hawkstone house. The day eased up towards noon and was hot. He didn't like riding in the heat. His barrel belly likely caused some discomfort for his horse, too. Over his striped shirt he wore a silk vest with the star badge prominent, while his pudgy hands held the reins. Cheek whiskers grew down from his temples to cover his sagging jowls. The hair had turned grey under his black bowler hat – too grey for a man not quite fifty, and not quite wealthy.

But he might have a second chance at wealth.

Ahead across the flat prairie he made out the shack against a shimmering horizon. He wondered if Anson Hawkstone had been there yet. The money surely waited where he had hidden it, unless Pine Oliver and Big Ears Kate had found the hiding place. There was something off-centre about that Pine Oliver – the marshal didn't think it was his real name, and he reckoned the polecat was there for more than a poke at Big Ears Kate in a convict's house – and maybe besides the hidden money. Yates had never met the man. Since it wasn't quite noon, Kate might still be in night clothes and he'd get a good look at what was big besides her ears.

The marshal election was coming up. He'd have to do the rounds again – glad handshake, buy merchants and the regular boys drinks to get their vote. He didn't mind because there were advantages to being town marshal. One thing was free breakfast at the café with that cute Suzy running about with the coffee pot, and an occasional free drink was offered at Slim's Saloon. For another he got a free poke with every new whore that came to town and joined the Gentlemen Kingdom run by Italian madam, Vicki Verona – usually real young and sure better looking than Vicki's usual crop of buffaloes.

Ahead he saw the house, with sunlight glaring against the front window. A tethered roan stood outside the door, its neck glistening in the noon-day sun from running.

The marshal rode close. 'Hello, the house!'

The door opened and Billy Bob Crutch stepped out. 'It's Marshal Yates from town.'

Billy Bob dressed trail hand, with a ten-gallon Stetson and wool vest, and his chest covered by a bright red kerchief. He carried double-draw Peacemakers. Half his left ear was missing. He was joined in front of the door by a slick, skinny gambler-type *hombre* with a weasel face and soft hands.

'Step on down, Marshal,' the *hombre* said. 'Come in for coffee.'

Billy Bob said, 'Marshal Leather Yates, mebbe you don't know him – this here is Pine Oliver. He's been staying with Kate, sorta keeping her company.'

As Marshal Yates swung down from the creaking saddle, he figured Pine carried an in-vest Derringer, as he did – no hip Colt like the marshal, though.

Yates stepped inside the house looking for Big Ears Kate in her bedclothes. Either Anson Hawkstone lived like a pig three years ago, or these two had added litter over the two years they had squatted in his shack – around a rough table and four chairs were clothes, dirty dishes, greasy stove, fly-specked windows, empty whiskey bottles, wadded newspaper, tobacco spit – he reckoned Big Ears Kate as not much of a housekeeper, and he wouldn't want howdy-do time or acquaintance conversation with her off the mattress. Some women affected a man that way. He decided not to sit – he stood just inside the door.

Billy Bob said, 'He come and got the money, Marshal. Sometime in the night he rode in and got a shovel someplace and dug it up and took it with him. We seen the hole out back at mid-morning – just a worm-eaten bank bag full of paper.'

'I thought I heard something,' Pine said.

The marshal took the cup of coffee. 'You didn't go see?'

'Kate was in one of her moods.'

Big Ears Kate parted the curtain from the bedroom wearing a tight, faded blue travelling dress that covered her from throat to ankle but could not hide her ample curves. Besides her oval peachy face with rouge cheeks, her dominant feature – besides those curves – was the wild, sagebrush, corn-shaded hair that fluffed out and down and not only covered her large ears but both sides of her face. She took a cup of coffee and nodded to the marshal. 'We might have been killed in our sleep, Marshal. That criminal was here to the house, digging out back by the pines – taking the money.'

'It's his house.' The marshal had his fill of looking at her. Wearing that dress, what good was she? He was there for a purpose and he figured he ought to get on with it. To all three he said, 'You know where he's staying, don't you?'

Billy Bob said, 'With the old Apache woman. I been watching the village. On my way into Wharton, I seen her and him come in in that old buckboard of hers. She picked him up from prison.'

Marshal Leather Yates took another sip of coffee, while his eyes looked back to stare at Kate. 'He's there with the money. Don't you think he'll come back to revisit parts of Kate?'

Pine took a step towards the marshal. 'That ain't there

for him. And for nobody else, neither.'

The marshal half smiled, as if the gambler-weasel thought he would actually make a move. There was something familiar about the polecat that he couldn't quite grab. He shrugged. 'Just sayin' somebody ought to go on over there and take that money away from him.'

'You go right ahead, Marshal,' Billy Bob said. 'The jasper's too mean for me. And he's got all them Apache around him. I don't intend to get myself scalped over money I don't know about. We never had chance to count or split the take. The bank told reporters fifty thousand. And no split. If the feds took twenty-five thousand, does that mean Hawkstone got another twenty-five? Or more? Or less? We don't know.'

'How come we don't know, Billy Bob?' Yates said.

'He got hisself captured and never said how much or where it might be.'

Leather Yates said, 'And how come he got hisself captured, Billy Bob?'

'Somebody shot off their big mouth to get freedom – One Eye Tim Brace or Wild Fletch Badger turned in poor Hawkstone to the feds so they could ride away free.'

'Who shot off their big mouth around Wharton City?'

Billy Bob blinked. 'You think it was *me*?'

Pine Oliver said, 'I'll get the money. I ain't afraid of no Anson Hawkstone.'

The marshal put his coffee cup down on one of the few table spaces, and frowned at Pine Oliver. 'Just who the hell are you?'

'I know I wasn't part of that robbery three years ago – but I'll be part of the next one coming up.'

Billy Bob stiffened. 'What next one?'

The marshal squinted. 'What do you know? *Who* do you know?'

Billy Bob looked back and forth, from Pine Oliver to the marshal, and shook his head. 'Look, whatever you fellas got cooking, you can just leave me out. My robbin' and killin' days is over. I got me a sweet live-in whore and I don't intend. . . .'

The marshal said, 'I don't intend, neither. . . .' He drew his Colt .45 Peacemaker and shot Billy Bob through the heart.

The gunshot cracked inside the small shack. Billy Bob's eyes widened as he jerked back, both hands over his bleeding chest. His ten-gallon hat flew off his balding head. Pine Oliver's hand started under his vest. Big Ears Kate swung her arm behind her, then immediately brought it forward with a small revolver. She'd have to be next. Without really aiming, Yates fired, hitting Kate through the throat. She spun around and dropped the pistol as she bent and folded head first. By then, Pine Oliver had apparently had a change of mind. He pulled his hand from the vest empty, and raised it with the other.

'I ain't drawin' on you, Marshal.'

Breathing heavily, Yates kept the Colt on him. 'You got maybe five seconds to tell me who you are, and what you been doing here with Kate.'

'Can we see if she's OK?'

'She ain't OK. She's bleeding quicker'n a hand pump – gone beyond to wherever unpaid whores like her go.'

'I got to see.'

'You just threw out three seconds. Two more and you're with her.'

'OK, I ain't Pine Oliver like I been tellin' everybody. My name is Boot Hobson.'

Yates squinted. The name sounded familiar, and the weasel face put with that name cleared the matter right up. 'I got a poster on you in my office – five hundred dollars.

You held up stages with Pearl Harp.'

'She's about to get released. We got somethin' workin' for when she gets here.'

'Boot Hobson,' Yates said.

'So what happens now, Marshal?'

'Now that we got a revenge killing here outta Hawkstone, I take you to jail and get my reward. Then we might rig an escape and talk about this thing you got with Pearl Harp. But right now you're goin' to help me burn this house to the ground. When them two bodies are cooled and crispy, you and me is gonna bury them so nobody knows until I'm ready. Hawkstone will get blamed. But first I'll take that pea shooter in your vest – nice and slow.'

'You might not want to haul me to jail just yet, Marshal,' Boot Hobson said. 'Let's have us a talk about what Pearl is bringing with her.'

# FIVE

Hawkstone saw the smoke as he rode towards the house. There were no more flames, only a charred black frame wiggling in the afternoon wind. High up, smoke wafted away as if it was tired.

He was concentrating so much on the house he didn't notice the man behind the first row of pines.

'Halt the pony, Hawkstone, or I'll blow you outta the saddle with this here scattergun.'

Hawkstone reined up and slowly turned to look at the pines. 'Who fired my house?'

'That'd be Marshal Leather Yates.'

'You the one called Pine Oliver?'

The man took a step out a little from the pines with the double-barrel twelve. 'First off, you ease that hogleg out of the holster. Use your thumb and finger. That's it, slow and easy. Drop it to the ground. To answer your question – I used to be Pine Oliver when I was with Kate. But I'm Boot Hobson, waitin' for Pearl Harp. You remember Pearl Harp? She sure remembers you.'

'So where is Big Ears Kate?'

'Dead and crispy – the marshal shot her down along with Billy Bob Crutch, then torched your house. We buried them behind me along the edge of the pines.'

'But he didn't shoot you.'

'I think he got plans for me – but enough about him and them others. Let's talk about how come your saddle-bags is so bulky.'

Hawkstone couldn't really see him clearly, just the business end of the double-barrel. It didn't matter. His Colt was down there on the ground. 'I got a tin box,' he said.

'Untie the bags and drop them to the ground. I'll have a look at the tin box and whatever is in the other one.'

'I can't do that,' Hawkstone said.

'Not a problem. I can do it myself after you're blown outta the saddle and on the ground yourself.'

Hawkstone said nothing. He sat in the saddle and stared at the shotgun barrels. He cursed himself for getting surprised by this weasel, who had probably killed Kate and burned down his house – and was now going to get the money. He twisted in the saddle and untied the saddle-bags and dropped them to the ground; the one with the tin box made a clang sound, the wood box in the other bag made no noise.

He said, 'You got one last chance, Boot Hobson. I'll have

to hunt you down and kill you.'

'Then I should drop you right here. Only I can't. Pearl took a liking to you. She come up with this plan and she wants you in it. I was never nothin' important to her – that's how come I rode off when it looked like the law was hot on us. She got a thing for you, though, Hawkstone. That's why I got to tell you to ride on out. Forget about comin' after me. Go on, now git.' He took a step forwards. 'Ah, hell, I can't let you out there on a horse. You really will come after me. I got to slow you down some.'

Hawkstone had turned away to ride off. The shot came from a derringer – small calibre, but with enough hitting power to slam his shoulder and knock him out of the saddle. He went forwards and down, and hit desert sand with his elbows first. His Stetson twirled away off his head. The chestnut reared and immediately took off at a run.

Hawkstone's first thought was to get back to his Colt, but stars swam through his head, a combination of the bullet and dropping from the saddle. He had a moment when he had to gather himself, get turned around and back to clear thinking. But it wasn't going to come fast enough. Hobson had quickly run from the pines and scooped up the saddle-bags, and run back again. He took a step to pick up Hawkstone's Colt, but apparently decided not to waste the time. His footsteps went back to the pines, and he rode away around the backside of the charred house skeleton.

And then he was gone.

Hawkstone crawled to his Peacemaker and got it in his grip. His shoulder burned with searing flame, bleeding badly. He looked beyond the smoking remains that had once been his house towards the pines. The galloping hoofs faded fast.

For Anson Hawkstone lying on desert scrub, normal thinking eased back slowly. The bullet had hit a little lower than his left shoulder, more a crease inside the upper arm. A patch of blood covered the spot and soaked down his shirt sleeve past his elbow. Afternoon sun baked down on him. His canteen was on his saddle, which was on the chestnut, which had probably run back to the Apache village corral. Somebody in the village would see and make a noise about it.

He rose up on his right elbow and looked at what was left of the black house skeleton. The sight didn't work him up enough to boil his blood. He had built the structure quick and dirty, as a place that offered more strength than a tepee or wickiup. It held no sentimental value for him, any more than Big Ears Kate had. She and it had been part of his outlaw life that he now wanted to ride away from. He'd served his time. He figured to be starting over – but that would have to be after the Boot Hobson fella was dealt with – and maybe Marshal Leather Yates, too. Hobson had to give up the money and die – Hawkstone's fresh start began with that money.

With no support to grab except sagebrush wiggling in the wind, he waited a bit before getting his boots under him and pushing to stand. A wave of dizziness washed over him, and he weaved like a straw scarecrow in a windy cornfield. He took a deep breath and his head cleared. With his right hand gripped on the wounded arm he stepped off in the direction of the Apache village.

It didn't take many steps to remind him that boot stirrup heels were never made for walking – they were made for riding, and that was what he should be doing. He fell into a stagger that had his head bobbing like a walking horse, his Stetson brim pulled low over his hazel eyes.

Hawkstone conjured up thoughts of Pearl Harp, the tiny, sometimes cute fellow prisoner at Yuma Territorial. The warden must have delivered on his promise if she was about to be released. She had a job planned. Since she held up stagecoaches it might be reckoned that that was what she had in mind. He tried to remember other prisoners who might be connected to stagecoaches, but couldn't. There was one mousy book-keeper type arrested for embezzling. He had worked for Longfellow Copper, the biggest copper-mining company in the territory. They were so big they had their own stagecoaches to run important men back and forth to the mines from Tucson.

But if Pearl thought Hawkstone was jumping into stage-coach holdups, she'd better pause and think again. Important men likely didn't carry much cash with them, so there had to be another reason.

The sun at his back cast long shadows. All he saw in front was more mesquite and plains – no creeks or rivers. The Rio Gila was to his right, but the hills were too rough to make it before dark. He stopped and sat with his legs crossed and breathed deep with his eyes closed.

The bank three years ago had been in Mineral City, two days' hard ride up the Colorado from Yuma. Hawkstone suspected Marshal Leather Yates had something to do with the planning, but the lawman wasn't with them. There were Billy Bob Crutch, One Eye Tim Brace, Wild Fletch Badger and Hawkstone. First off, inside the bank, Wild Fletch had shot and killed the girl teller, Gertie Sump. That changed the attitude of the town. The boys got the cash, but had a spray of bullets zinging about as they tried to get out of town. Hawkstone took one in the calf. Billy Bob caught a head shot that took off half his left ear. One Eye Tim was hit along the neck and in the butt. Wild Fletch who killed the girl got off without a skin break.

They rode hard due east away from the Colorado, no idea how much cash they got. One Eye Tim and Billy Bob were bleeding bad and demanded attention. Before dark, Federal Marshal Casey Steel and fifteen deputies were on their tails. Hawkstone kept the calf wrapped tight and his horse was faster. The other boys headed northeast towards Deep Well, while Hawkstone, once he saw the posse had a bead on the others, veered southeast for North Bend. From there he worked his way down to the Rio Gila and the Apache village and his house where Big Ears Kate waited. He counted his grab at ten thousand dollars, and buried it out back beyond the string of pines. Two days later Federal Marshal Casey Steel came with twin pearl-handled Colts drawn, and arrested him. The other three fellas never went to jail.

Hawkstone sat in the sand with his legs crossed, shaking his head. They had turned on him and had given him up to get their own freedom – had even said he killed the teller, though nobody could prove that. He didn't know if Leather Yates had been part of the robbery and decided who went free and who went to prison. He also didn't know if Big Ears Kate had been part of his capture.

*False friends and shadows show only when the sun shines.*

Remembering Ben Franklin, Hawkstone thought he sure could use a drink of water.

He looked up to see shimmering forms off in the distance. The shadows came towards him. He stared from under the brim of his Stetson.

It was Black Feather riding his pinto with the chestnut mare in tow.

## SIX

The old woman and Hattie fussed over him in the wickiup. Hawkstone had a yellow cotton shirt as backup: he owned three shirts – one on, one clean, one ready for washing – in three colours, blue, brown and yellow. Hattie would wash and sew the bullet tear in the blue shirt while he wore the yellow. His main thought was that they had lost the daylight.

After supper, down by Disappointment Creek, Hawkstone and Black Feather sat on boulders beside the bubbling stream. They rolled Bull Durham tobacco in corn-skin paper, and fired up smokes while passing a whiskey bottle back and forth. Tommy Wolfinger stopped for a sip of fire water and a short talk to welcome Hawkstone back to the tribe. He was Black Feather's age, tall and lithe, thin as a pine, and had no use for the tobacco habit. He and Black Feather often hunted together, and with Burning Buffalo he competed for Hattie's charms – neither considered Hawkstone as competition, believing that the former outlaw was far too old and creaky for a frisky, willowy princess. Tommy left them alone after one drink.

'We leave at first light,' Black Feather said.

'Can you track him after half a day?'

'From what I see at the pines he is clumsy. He walks through life sloppy, with much noise. Yes, we will find him.'

'I'll have to kill him.'

Black Feather drank a swallow. 'You must do what you must do.'

Hawkstone took the bottle. He flipped his spent smoke into the creek. 'He might lead us around – maybe even as far as Tucson.'

'We will find him. The arm is painful and you are getting old. You better rest,' Black Feather said.

Hawkstone followed Black Feather up along the shore of Disappointment Creek. They veered west across the plain until they reached the charred lumps that were once his house. Black Feather studied the ground at the pines. He eased his pony around the perimeter of the tree trunks until he reached where Hobson had mounted and had immediately spurred his horse to a gallop.

He looked up slightly, then stared off into the Pinon Llano mountains angled to the right. 'He rode around the pines and the house on the side away from you. He headed for the Rio Gila river. That is the way we go.'

When they reached the Rio Gila, the sun had arched almost to a peak. Black Feather searched along the cottonwoods until he found the crossing, and they splashed across to where Hobson had scrambled up the opposite bank. They followed the trail along the river bank.

'He makes it easy,' Hawkstone said.

Black Feather let his sight move ahead along the bank. 'He is stupid, or he doesn't care who follows. Perhaps he thought you were dead.'

'I prefer that he's stupid. *Stupid hates smart – in others.*'

'Is that a Ben Franklin?'

'Don't rightly remember – mebbe.' Hawkstone jerked as he felt a prick of pain through his upper arm, and he grimaced, a gesture not unnoticed by Black Feather. Nothing went unnoticed by Black Feather.

'We will rest.'

'Why? You don't need rest.'

'The old man in you does,' Black Feather said. 'Three years is too long to be away for a man past forty.'

They swung down from their ponies among cottonwoods, and sat next to the flowing water with their backs against the trees. The shade felt good. They ate some jerky. They each had a swallow of whiskey from Hawkstone's bundle, and followed it with water. They each rolled a cigarette.

Hawkstone said, 'You figure where he's headed?'

'Not yet. We are close to the main trail – the old General Keambevs route that joins the Santa Fe trail.'

'Maybe he'll just swing back to Wharton.'

'Maybe – but you cannot kill him in Wharton City.'

'I can if I take out Marshal Leather Yates with him.'

'I think this *hombre* has other plans. If he crosses the Rio Gila again, I will know better.'

Late afternoon shadows spread long when the trail once again crossed the Rio Gila river. It was close to Williams Fork that flowed from the northeast.

When they lost the light, Hawkstone and his blood brother made camp. They built up their wool blankets next to a campfire, but actually slept apart on opposite sides of the creek. Hawkstone did not sleep well – he was too alert for any sound. Maybe Hobson knew they were dogging him. Doubtful, but the polecat might still double back and dry-gulch them.

Though tired, Hawkstone was grateful for the first sights and sounds of dawn, everything living wet with dew. He and Black Feather did not speak as they broke camp and saddled their mounts, and took up the trail once again. The trail continued leading north, up beyond Williams Fork towards Rio Salinas. They passed craggy mesas and rolling grass and mesquite, and rain-carved arroyos. Clouds kept the sun from glaring. After noon, once along Salt Creek, Black Feather spoke for the first time that day.

'He rides towards New Mexico Territory – down to Rio San Carlos.'

Hawkstone said, 'There's a stage station outside Fort Webster.'

'He might head there. There are copper mines above Fort Webster in New Mexico.'

They sat their mounts on a bluff looking down into New Mexico Territory.

Hawkstone rubbed his jowls. 'Why would he care about copper mines? Let's find out if he stopped at the stage-coach station.'

Black Feather gave Hawkstone a quizzical look.

Hawkstone stared down from the bluff. 'Boot Hobson used to run with the woman now in prison, Pearl Harp. She's about to get herself released. They held up stage-coaches.'

About ten miles before they reached Fort Webster, they came on the stage stop during a change of horses. A boy around sixteen had his hands full switching teams.

Hawkstone said, 'Need help with hitching?'

'My pa is supposed to be helpin'.'

'He ain't around. You want to wait or get it done?'

'Let's get it done.'

Hawkstone tagged the lad as a decision maker with a decent head on his shoulders.

With the three of them working, the horses snorting and stomping and kicking up dirt, they got the team hitched, and while the boy grinned his thanks, Hawkstone and Black Feather washed their hands, face and necks in the horse trough. Passengers standing on the porch watching had gone inside once the entertainment ended.

'What's your name, son?' Hawkstone asked.

'Sled.' He had tousled brown hair and wore no shoes. 'Wanna thank you fellas for the help.'

Hawkstone put his hand on the lad's shoulder. 'Who are your people inside?'

'Cauley, my pa, runs the station. My ma, Rose-Marie, does cookin' and cleanin'; she's helped by my sister, Char – short for Charlotte. She's fourteen.'

They were on the porch, stepping inside. Three men sat around a table with a clay bottle labelled 'corn-liquor' in the middle. They each had a glass. They were a dressy trio, in beige and tan suits with blue ties and short-brimmed east coast hats. A squatty *hombre* with a Montana Peak Stetson stood at a counter reaching up past his waist, settling money with the worried man on the other side. The worried man wore no hat, and Hawkstone took him to be Cauley. A slim, worn-looking woman with little colour to her face came from the back wiping her hands on an apron: Rose-Marie, and she looked worried, too.

Sled went out of the room.

'Stop that, Sled!' A girl cried from behind the wall.

Sled came back with a grin and an oatmeal cookie.

'Cauley, send Char out with some of them cookies,' a man from the table said. He had a fleshy face and sat straight and tall, looking around as if he was in charge.

The squat Montana Peak Stetson at the counter said, 'Time to roll out, gents.' He nodded to the man who had spoken. 'Mr Brennen?'

'After an oatmeal cookie,' Brennen said. 'Get on out here, little darlin'. I bet you made them cookies with your own sweet hands.'

Char came out carrying a tray piled with the cookies. She looked older than her fourteen years, with charcoal hair in ringlets to her waist, and a short pink calico dress clinging over her filled frame, ending at her knees.

Hawkstone and Black Feather dragged chairs to a table the opposite side of the room. Besides the counter, the room only held tables and chairs. A painting of a clipper ship at sea hung on the wall across from the open door. The three men weren't interested in what hung on the wall – their attention was drawn to Char and that calico dress and her oatmeal cookies.

Outside the open door the four-horse team stomped and snorted against billowing dirt. One whinnied with impatience.

The squat Montana Peak Stetson said, 'We're rollin', gents!'

Brennen said, 'I say when we roll.' He forced his gaze

from Char, who set the tray on the table and skittered away, to the table where Hawkstone and Black Feather sat. 'What the hell is an Injun doing in your place, Cauley? He ought to be out in the dirt with the horses. You don't allow no redskins in here.'

Sled had been leaning against the counter across from his pa munching a cookie. 'He helped with the horses. He got a right.'

'The hell he does,' Brennen said. He pushed his chair back to stand.

A moment of silence floated across the room – only the sounds of harness jangling and horses stomping outside reached them.

Hawkstone said, louder than he needed to, 'Hombre, don't let your running mouth get you killed.'

Brennen stood and glared at him. The other two men turned for a look.

'Do you know who I am?' Brennen said.

'Ain't important who you are – I know *what* you are.'

'I am *Mister* Brennen, Vice-President of Operations for the Longfellow Copper Mining Company.'

'That's a mouthful, fella.'

'What's your name?'

'Sidewinder Slick from Rolling Rock Crick,' Hawkstone said.

Brennen dismissed Hawkstone with a wave of his hand. 'Let's move out, men – nothing but idiots in here.'

With scraping chairs the other two stood, and after loading their pockets with cookies, headed for the open door. The squat driver was already outside.

As Brennen passed by Hawkstone and Black Feather, he said, 'This ain't over, boy.'

'Probably not,' Hawkstone said, 'seeing as how you're so weary of living.'

# SEVEN

After the stagecoach rolled out, Black Feather pulled his ten inch-blade bowie knife from under the table and slipped it back in its sheath.

Hawkstone leaned back with a stare. 'You figure to gut him like a pig?' He jerked with a grimace of arm pain.

'Only if he begged me to – and he tumbled down that road.' He showed a mask without expression, straight raven hair to his shoulders held by a beaded forehead band.

Sled went back in the kitchen, likely for another cookie. Cauley brought a clay bottle of corn-liquor to the table with three glasses, and sat between the two men. 'Fella brings this stuff over by the case three times a month – I can hardly keep it in stock, what with the army soldiers from the fort. Sorry about the one with the bad manners. I shoulda been helping the boy, but they was arguing price. *Them*, kickin' a fuss, and they could buy this place with one week's pay. You boys drifting through?' He had a week's beard, mussed hair, and his clothes were dirty. Black fingernails scratched under his armpit.

'Looking for a fella,' Hawkstone said.

Cauley glanced from one to the other, rested his gaze on Black Feather. 'You know how folks think in these parts. You really shouldn't be in here.' Cauley took his time pouring each glass three-quarters full.

Hawkstone said, 'You want us to leave?'

'Not you – you're OK. It's just, I got a business here.'

Hawkstone looked around the empty room. 'You feed

off the copper mines, don't you?'

The first swallow of the juice went down with the kick of a buffalo, and almost strangled him. Hawkstone felt his eyes water. It took some seconds to get feeling back to his throat.

Cauley sat back with tight lips. 'Yeah, most of my business comes from the mines. The stage runs the payroll from Tucson by way of Fort Webster.'

Hawkstone nodded towards the open door. Sand and dirt blew in lightly across the floor. 'That stage have payroll?'

'Don't carry payroll and important men on the same stage.'

'Is that what them were, important men?'

'Just ask 'em.'

Hawkstone took another small swallow of the corn licker. He pulled out Bull Durham tobacco and corn-skin paper for rolling smokes, and handed them round. When the three men were lit, Char came with another tray of oatmeal cookies, then quickly scurried out of the room. She carried the face of a child with the body of a developed woman. Hawkstone understood the interest of men. He looked at Cauley. 'Any strangers stop in – say, yesterday or the day before? This would be a weasel gambler, rodent-looking type, eyes close together, maybe noticing things he got no business noticing.'

'Like my daughter?'

'Or your cash drawer.'

Cauley blew smoke to the ceiling. 'Yeah, he was here. Yesterday afternoon. He asked about stagecoaches like you – stagecoaches and payrolls. But he was like Brennen – undressing my little girl with his eyes. We had a real short conversation. I told him nothing.'

Hawkstone put his elbows on the table. 'You talk like your girl is some problem.'

'She's a lot of problem. Them soldier boys from Fort Webster ride the ten miles to get a snoot full of this here corn liquor. Saturday night, they drink and argue and dance and hug with Char – anything to get their hands on her. They try to sweet-talk her and give her trinkets.' He shook his head. 'The girl is only fourteen. She gets influenced and believes their chatter. I try to keep her away, but them cavalry riders sniff her out like she's in season. It's all I can do to try to keep her innocent – if she still is. Sometimes I wish one of them would sweep her away and marry her so I can get some sleep at night.'

Hawkstone took another sip of liquor. Black Feather kept to himself as always. They stared at the cookies, nobody taking one. Hawkstone said, 'His name is Boot Hobson. What did you tell him about stagecoaches and payrolls, Cauley?'

'Like I said, we had a short conversation. I kept Char back in the kitchen. He asked a lot of questions.'

'Like what?'

'Like, how many coaches a month roll through to the mines? I told him, two a month. And, was there another road that bypassed this station? I didn't know. Might other coaches be taking the payroll, say along another road someplace? I got no idea. And, what day of the week did the stage roll through? Every other Wednesday. Did any of them have extra guards? Sometimes I saw a couple mounted men with rifles. And that was it.'

Hawkstone nodded. 'You got any idea how big the payroll is?'

'Just guesses, from army soldiers.'

'About how big?'

'About fifty thousand a load, plus or minus a few thousand.'

Black Feather cleared his throat. He looked out of the

open door where sand and dirt blew. 'The trail goes bad,' he said. 'We here too long.'

Hawkstone dropped the butt of the cigarette in the liquor glass. He stood and took Cauley's hand. 'Much obliged.'

Black Feather was already at the door.

'You want a young wife?' Cauley asked.

'I'm too young to get married,' Hawkstone said.

It took five minutes away from the station for Black Feather to pick up Boot Hobson's trail again. They rode slowly beside each other.

Black Feather said, 'You got no Ben Franklin?'

'About what?'

'About two girls maybe to be your woman.'

Hawkstone said, '*When there's marriage without love, there will be love without marriage.*'

'Good one,' Black Feather said with a chuckle. 'Maybe you *are* too young to get married.'

'Or too old.'

'Does the trail wear on you?'

'My arm stings. Do you know where he rides?'

'Not yet.'

Hawkstone shifted position in the saddle. 'When you have an idea, I'd like to see if more roads go to the Longfellow mines. The company might send wagons or buggies on a Tuesday along a different route – or a Thursday – a day before or after the Wednesday stage-coach.'

'Out of Tucson?'

'Or Wharton City.'

Black Feather leaned out to study the trail. 'You want to postpone the thief?'

'No, I want my money back. I remember there was an

embezzler inside, from the Longfellow outfit. Maybe he knew when the payroll was really sent, and maybe he told Pearl about it to get some touch-feel-kiss favours from her. I can't remember his name. Once Pearl turned on her charms, he'd pretty much give her anything she wanted.'

'Like you did?'

'I had nothing to give her 'cept my own charm.'

They rode along in silence. Black Feather said, 'When the woman is out, will you run with her?'

'I'm done with that robbing, killing, outlaw life. I might have a talk with the Longfellow bankers in Tucson. I might see if they got a finder's fee for stolen booty.'

Black Feather reined up to halt. 'We can look for other stage roads now.'

'You know where he's headed?'

Black Feather pointed. 'Look where the trail leads, the broken mesquite. See the cigarette butt, the horseshoe prints? One nail through the hoof was not clinched tight. The head leaves a dimple in the ground. It is deeper in mud. He rides back to the General Keambevs route. You were right. The route goes by Wharton City. That is where he moves.'

# EIGHT

Town marshal Leather Yates, propped up on pillows, breathed heavily from effort. 'That was real fine, Tippy. You're going to be good at this. How old are you?'

'Seventeen.' She was still slender, with smooth skin and

a baby cherub face, her brown hair hanging to her tiny butt. It might take a year or two for her to start puffing with bed lumps and wearing out like an old saddle. She shook her head. 'I din' want my daddy to sell me. I don' wanna do this,' she said.

'He must have needed the money. We'll have a drink then fool around some more.'

'No more freebies,' she said. 'Vicki says you get one jump free, no more. You got to pay the two dollars if you want more.'

'Now, Tippy, little darlin', I'm the town marshal. I'm special.'

'You're special fat. I don't like fat. You better leave my room now. I don't want you no more again.'

Yates reached for her but she danced across the room with a scowl.

'Get back in bed,' he said.

She had put on a frilly robe. 'I'm going downstairs. Leave my room or I call Vicki. She will ban you from Gentlemen Kingdom. You're too fat and you want too much free.' Tippy scuttled out of the door and was gone.

Ten miles west of Wharton City sat the Way Out Saloon, a twenty-foot lean-to with home-built tree-limb chairs and a plank bar – no mirrors, no fancy women, no selection in whiskey. The skinny, shrivelled owner, Rocky Face Fiona, in her mid-forties, took over when her husband, Tank the Whiskey Maker, was shot dead during a robbery. Her face looked like a rocky surface patch along a desert trail, and she acted as if she didn't much mind the name. Rocky had the recipe for making whiskey, and continued to make it and sell it at the saloon.

Way Out Saloon was a good place to meet for those who wanted to avoid a lot of attention – or for a town marshal who didn't want good citizens to see the kind of riff-raff he had to mix with. And Fiona was beholden to the marshal, since he had never charged Tank, or her, any tax on the whiskey they made and sold. Even when he helped himself to parts of her, he made her know she was still beholden and owed him.

'I got to arrest you now, Boot,' Marshal Yates said.

They sat on spindly chairs, hunched over a planked table. Four other men were huddled on the other side of the shack. The cracked floor was peppered with tobacco spit.

Boot Hobson made a sour face when he gulped half a glass of Rocky's concoction. 'I tell you, I got the money. I took Hawkstone's buried stash – ten thousand dollars – got the saddle-bags out there on my horse.'

'You didn't hide it?'

'He ain't coming after it. I think he died and cooked out there on the prairie after I shot him. His horse run off and he was all alone.'

'So I got to arrest you for shooting down Anson Hawkstone, and get the reward for your other past crimes.'

'Not with Pearl Harp coming to town.'

'She'll be real upset if Hawkstone is dead.'

'Well, I *think* he's dead. I took off, so I really don't know.'

'Took off where?'

Hobson hunched his shoulders. 'Last letter I got from Pearl, she says she's hooked up with this jasper, Roscoe Dees, who stole that money on the books from Longfellow Copper. She writes Roscoe knows about secret stagecoaches or wagons or buggies carrying lots of cash – payroll cash, from the bank to the mines. She ain't got all the facts yet, but says she's humpin' like a fresh-caught fish on shore to get the rest outta him.'

Yates let a swallow of the Rocky juice burn its way down. 'She say if this Roscoe wants in as part of what we got to do?'

'Never did. Nope, never did write nothing about that. One thing she wrote twice – Hawkstone got to be part of what we do.'

'He can't if he's dead.'

'We got to find that out.'

'Not you, you're off to jail – under arrest.'

'Only until you get the reward money, right?'

'Depends on what Pearl has to tell us. I'll be picking her up at the Tucson station tomorrow evening.' Yates rubbed a chubby hand over his jiggling, grey-whiskered jowls. 'Thing is, if Hawkstone is alive. . . .'

Boot Hobson nodded and looked across the room. 'Well, you got to find that out on account of I'll be in jail, under arrest.'

'That'll only be until I send a wire off for the reward. Once I got confirmation, you'll hook up with me and Pearl and maybe this Roscoe Dees fella.'

'What about One-Eye Tim Brace and Wild Fletch Badger?'

'Yeah, them too. Now, you know I can't be taking part in no actual stagecoach hold-up – after all, I'm the marshal of Wharton City. I got an image to protect.'

'Sure. And you got an election coming up.'

'Exactly. And if Hawkstone is still with us, we got to give him his money back.'

'Dammit, Marshal, I don't like that. I know you're trying to get him to throw in with us, but. . . .'

'It don't matter to you on account of I'm confiscating the saddle-bags right here. I'll see he gets it nice and friendly.'

'I want it.'

' 'Course you do. And you'll be able to grab it after he gets shot dead at the hold-up, being the outlaw he's always been.'

Hobson sat back. 'Huh?'

'Only Pearl wants him with us, nobody else. She might have trouble surviving herself. No, if Hawkstone is alive, he'll get shot down during the stagecoach hold-up.'

'And that ain't all you got planned, is it, Yates?'

'No, it ain't,' Leather Yates said.

# NINE

When Hawkstone and Black Feather rode into Wharton City, they headed straight for the marshal's office. They learned the marshal had business west of town – off the main road, something about stolen money in saddle-bags.

They rode out at a gallop.

Black Feather circled behind Way Out Saloon while Hawkstone reined in next to a roan which had his saddle-bags tied to the back of its saddle. He swung down from the chestnut, unhooking the thong holding the hammer of his Colt Peacemaker .45 as he did so. He felt a stitch of pain in his arm. He patted the roan on the rump, then started to untie the saddle-bags.

Marshal Leather Yates and Boot Hobson came out of the curtain doorway, with Hobson in front. Hawkstone had his hand on the Peacemaker. He had one more leather tie holding the bags.

'Hey!' Hobson croaked.

Hawkstone pulled and rested the butt of the Colt on the saddle seat. 'Stand easy. I won't shoot you dead 'til I get my goods.' He aimed from Hobson to the marshal and back again.

The marshal said, 'Put the gun away, Hawkstone. I just arrested this jasper.' Yates's fat face was flushed with the impact of Rocky's whiskey.

Hawkstone kept the .45 aimed. 'That so? Which of you killed Big Ears Kate and burned down my house?'

'Don't know nothing about that,' Yates said.

Hawkstone aimed at Boot Hobson. 'That leaves you.' The fingers of his left hand still worked the last knot on his saddle-bags.

'No, it wasn't me.' Hobson glanced at the marshal.

'One of you did, or both.' Hawkstone saw Black Feather ease along the side of the saloon, his '76 Winchester at the ready.

Marshal Leather Yates said, 'Now Hawkstone, you just go right ahead and take that money. I was gonna give it back to you anyway, right after I got this outlaw behind bars.'

Hawkstone knew the only shot that either had to him was from his chest up, as the horse and saddle was a barrier. But he wanted to make sure the money was still there. 'Marshal, slip your hands down the front of your gun belt. Keep your thumbs outside. Your belly will help hold them there.'

Hobson took a step back. 'This ain't gonna figure for me.' His hand went to his Colt.

Hawkstone shot him in the chest, cocked the gun and shot him there again. The gunshots echoed off close hills and far mountains, while white smoke surrounded them. Hobson's forehead wrinkled with irritation as he dropped the Colt and bounced back against the front wall of the saloon. He slid to his knees, and fell face down in the desert sand.

The marshal tried to free his right hand from his belt. Keeping the Colt resting on the saddle, Hawkstone swung its aim to his big belly. 'Are you sure?' he said.

Black Feather slid around the corner of the shack and

poked his Winchester into the marshal's back. 'Not today,' he said.

The marshal stood stiff, glaring at Hawkstone, while Black Feather slid the lawman's Colt from its holster and threw it off among mesquite.

From inside the shack, Rocky shouted, 'You drunks take that noisy action away, off to the desert someplace – get it away from my business establishment.'

'Mount up, Marshal,' Hawkstone said.

'Mount up for where? I need that body to get my reward.'

'It might still be here when you swing back this way.'

Hawkstone pulled his saddle-bags from the roan and tied them to the back of his own saddle.

When the three men were mounted they walked their horses west down the road, Hawkstone in the lead, the marshal, and Black Feather behind with the Winchester in the crook of his arm.

After an hour, Hawkstone led the parade off the main trail and into raw sagebrush country with short, thick brown grass and mesquite and junipers all about.

'I'm a lawman,' Yates said. 'A town marshal.'

Hawkstone half-turned in the saddle. 'That supposed to impress me? You set up the bank job three years ago. I think you torched my house and shot Big Ears Kate. She might have been shallow on true affection and loyalty, but she was kind of a good old gal – soft on a cold winter's night. She didn't deserve to be gunned down.'

'It's complicated,' the marshal said.

'The hell you say. Uncomplicate it.'

'Pearl Harp is coming in on the Tucson train tomorrow. She may have this *hombre*, Roscoe Dees, with her. They know how bankers and copper-mine ramrods set up payroll stage-coach deliveries. Set them up and deliver so nobody knows.'

'That ain't got nothing to do with me,' Hawkstone said. 'I'm done with that life.'

'You figure to take your money and ride off someplace?'

'That's exactly what I figure.'

'Pearl wants you in on this. It don't help you killing Hobson, her old partner.'

'I ain't in the business of help.'

Another hour of walking the horses along, they were at a shallow canyon. They dismounted. Black Feather stood off, the rifle still on the marshal.

'You can't just kill a town marshal, Hawkstone. Killing a lawman will send a big posse after you. I can fix up the Hobson killing – say I done it 'cause he was resisting arrest. I'll do it, too. You got no blame in it. And I'll get the reward. You come in with Pearl and the rest of us, I'll see you got no connection to the killing – hell, I'll fix it so you weren't even there.'

Hawkstone rubbed his chin. 'Sounds good, but I ain't got no trust. Hobson had to go, not only 'cause he took my money, but he shot me and left me hot and dry – couldn't let that dangle out there without doing somethin'.' He turned to Black Feather. 'What you think, my brother?'

'Can't believe this one.'

'And that's the twist of it. Marshal, you just can't be trusted. I'll have to get back to you on your plan.'

Yates said, 'Let's call it a one-time offer.'

'Take off your clothes,' Hawkstone said.

'What?'

'Either that or the Apache here will shoot your foot.'

Leather Yates pulled everything off except his boots. He smelled in the clean air like a cavalry latrine. Black Feather stepped upwind, keeping the Winchester pointed to the flabby, fish-white belly.

'Boots, too,' Hawkstone said. He tied the smelly clothes

together, and straddled them across the marshal's horse's saddle. 'We'll be taking your pony along with us – leave him at the Way Out Saloon. We'll keep your boots, though. You'll have a hard walk but you'll probably make it.'

'You can't do this,' Yates cried. 'At least leave me my boots.'

Hawkstone and Black Feather mounted.

Hawkstone took the reins of the marshal's horse. 'I leave you with the words of an old friend – as best as I can remember.'

'Ben Franklin,' Black Feather said with a smile.

'*Let no pleasure tempt, no profit allure, no ambition corrupt, no example sway, no persuasion move you to do anything you know to be evil – that way you will always live jolly.*'

# TEN

Anson Hawkstone and Black Feather rode easy towards the Apache village, less than five miles out. The sun was setting and cast a scarlet spray across the landscape. Hawkstone didn't carry good feelings about shooting down Boot Hobson, but the outlaw had shot him, and he felt satisfied now that he had his money back. He reckoned he might regret not doing the same to the marshal.

Black Feather said, 'You churn inside – it shows on your face.'

'What if pony soldiers from Fort Grant rode in to shoot up the village?'

'Why would they?'

Hawkstone said, 'Suppose they been enticed? Suppose

somebody told them something to set 'em off, stir 'em up?'

Black Feather frowned. 'Who? What?'

'Say some fellas want a man to do something he don't want to do. Say they got no more tricks to use against him, and he keeps saying no. What trail do they take?'

Black Feather pondered as the horses stepped along side by side. 'They go after what's his – what he cares about – those he worries over. They hold a gun to the head of the innocent.'

'Lawmen think I don't care about nobody or nothing.'

'Not true. And that makes you vulnerable. There is the old woman and Hattie.'

'And you, and Burning Buffalo, and Tommy Wolfinger – and the children and old folks. There are too many.'

With just enough light to see the trail, they rode in silence for a spell.

'You have a path to track,' Black Feather said, making it in a statement, not a question.

Hawkstone said, 'I'm leaving the money with you. Tomorrow, early, I ride to Tucson.'

'We ride together.'

'No, you prepare the village for trouble. Most important, you show a path of protection for the old woman and Hattie.'

'You intend Hattie to be your woman?'

'She is like my young sister, but she is fodder for too many hungry fangs. In an attack she will be shredded of all innocence through every part of her.'

'You are certain of an attack?'

'I am certain of nothing, my brother. They want me as part of the hold-up. I'm thinking I got to do it, if they touch what I love.'

The old woman fixed rabbit, one of three that Burning Buffalo had shot and dropped at the wickiup door for

Hattie. Hawkstone reckoned Burning Buffalo was the front suitor for her, and probably the best choice. When darkness came, and after food and water had been taken, Hawkstone met Burning Buffalo, Tommy Wolfinger and Black Feather along the bank of Disappointment Creek for whiskey and cigarettes, and talk.

Burning Buffalo lightly rubbed the lance scar along his left cheek. He tossed his long pigtail over his shoulder to hang down his back. Tommy Wolfinger turned down the offer of makings. At twenty-three, he looked lithe as a boy, with straight black hair. Like Burning Buffalo, he carried a Remington tucked in a belt around his buckskin. While both braves competed for the attention of Hattie Smooth Water, they carried no animosity towards each other.

Moonlight winked silver over the slosh of the creek, moonlight sharp and shiny as a knife blade. Shadows of cottonwood surrounded them. They sat on boulders the size of buffalo. Black Feather took a pull from the whiskey bottle and handed it to Hawkstone.

'The cavalry got no gripe with us,' he said.

Hawkstone drank and passed the bottle to Tommy Wolfinger. 'A big payroll stagecoach hold-up with word the money is here might fire 'em off. Longfellow Copper Mining is big medicine – might roust out fifteen pony soldiers to come stampeding down on this village.'

'We will move village,' Tommy said. 'We are only a band of thirty humans – mostly women and little ones – we cannot fight so many.'

'I got to find out more first,' Hawkstone said. 'Day after tomorrow, you meet me in Tucson. All of you, dress like white men – heavy coats to cover your hair, cowboy hats, boots, ride with saddles. Be ready to do some hold-up.'

'Rider coming,' Black Feather said.

Hawkstone dropped the empty whiskey bottle in the

creek. The three braves moved off silently, watching the rider come in, the rider sitting tall in the saddle, looking around as if he owned the land around him, and the village, and the people in it.

'Anson Hawkstone,' the rider said. One of his pearl-handled Peacemakers glinted in the moonlight. 'Let's go for a night ride.'

'Federal Marshal Casey Steel, you on a kill raid?' Hawkstone said.

The marshal waited silently while Hawkstone saddled the chestnut mare. They rode from the village at a slow walk, moving in the direction of the burned house a mile away. Steel's face was hidden from moonlight by the black Montana Peak Stetson pulled low over his eyes, a shadow with endless other shadows. His stocky frame rested easily in the saddle. Hawkstone had no intention of drawing down on a United States Federal Marshal.

Steel said, 'Fresh outta prison and already in trouble. You hard cases never learn.'

'What trouble?'

'You made Leather Yates trek three miles back from the desert buck naked, cooked medium rare. You even kept his boots – that's serious, keeping a man's boots. He told me how you took your stolen saddle-bags after he shot Boot Hobson trying to escape capture. What's in them bags?'

'Personal things.'

'Uh huh, whatever happened to Big Ears Kate?'

'Took off with a fella, I hear.'

'Ain't seen nothing of Billy Bob Crutch, neither. You reckon they run off together?'

'Mebbe – after burnin' down my house.'

'She didn't exactly pine away for you over them three years. I hear she shared feathers with Boot Hobson, who

was callin' himself Pine Oliver at the time. Now what's inter-
estin' to me is he was the same Boot Hobson used to run
with Pearl Harp – her just fresh released from Yuma
Territorial and on a train comin' to Tucson. Is that inter-
estin' to you, Anson Hawkstone?'

'Hobson is recently deceased. Their runnin' together
days are done.'

'You gonna meet her at the station?'

'Maybe Marshal Yates will take care of that.'

'Why you reckon she's coming to Tucson?'

'I don't reckon.'

Steel came out quick with it. 'You dig up the money yet?'

'What money?'

The tall black Stetson nodded. 'Yeah, you got it, got it
hid someplace else now.'

'Marshal, I'm just trying to get settled after long, bad
prison time.'

'What you hear from One-Eye Tim Brace and Wild
Fletch Badger?'

'Nothing.'

'I hear tell they in Tucson. If you go there, I'll figure the
old gang is gettin' together again for some action. You
coming to town, Hawkstone?'

## ELEVEN

Pearl Harp stepped down from the stagecoach with a
helping hand from the man riding shotgun. It would still be
many months before train tracks reached the new station

platform in Tucson, expected sometime before 1880. City fathers – including the young rich banker, Barron Jacobs – told newspapers Tucson would become more civilized with the coming of the train. He'd seen it in other towns where his family had built banks. These days Tucson was just as rowdy, filthy, noisy and deadly as that silver mining camp town, Tombstone, to the south.

For now, at tracks end, sixty miles north in Casa Grande, passengers were shuttled by fast stagecoach along a well-used track road to the downtown station. Pearl thought to see Boot Hobson waiting for her. The air wasn't warm, the sun keeping a low glare with a cold wind heralding the coming winter.

From Yuma Prison she had hired a wagon to take her into Yuma, where money wired from her parents waited. Pearl bought a long-skirt chemise, and grey serge travelling dress and jacket, and heeled shoes. Inside the small carpet bag, along with a split riding skirt and boots and buckskin pants, and unmentionables, she kept a Remington .36 revolver. Another weapon, an eleven-ounce, double-barrel, single-action Remington .41 derringer, cost her eight dollars, and she carried it in a small pocket towards the back of her dress. She wore no bonnet. A decent range hat had to be available in a town the size of Tucson.

Off the stage, standing on the boardwalk holding the handle of her carpet bag, she watched a flush-faced, rotund city marshal sidle up to her.

He tipped his hat brim. 'Pearl Harp? Marshal Leather Yates, at your service.'

'I got to check in with you?'

'Oh, no, I'm marshal of Wharton City, not Tucson. This greeting is personal. I got to tell you about the demise of your friend, Boot Hobson – gunned down by that back-shooting outlaw, Anson Hawkstone.'

'So you say. My affection for Anson Hawkstone runs a little deeper than it did for Boot Hobson. I understand Boot habituated with Big Ears Kate in Hawkstone's bed instead of her visiting Anson – he even changed his name.'

'True, true – here, let me take that bag.'

'The bag is fine. Where can I get me a hotel room?'

'I got a reservation at the Orndorff Hotel. A coupla boys are waiting for us. You travellin' alone?'

'Roscoe rides in tomorrow, bringin' my horse. He left a few days before me. The boys can stew for a day. How many you figure we got?'

'For what?'

'Boot and me wrote back and forth – and I had long pillow talk with Anson Hawkstone while we were in prison – so I know you ain't no honest marshal. You planned the bank up there in Mineral City three years ago, and you want to ramrod this.'

The marshal squinted. 'You got a problem with that?'

'How many we got?'

They began walking down the boardwalk toward the hotel, the marshal partly limping and shuffling and waddling in sunburn pain. Pearl didn't ask about his pain because she didn't care. She noticed glances from men. She figured the dress was too tight in the waist and bodice – men liked to guess what was under. She wouldn't be giving any intimate favours in Tucson. She'd keep giving it up to Roscoe, or switch over for Anson Hawkstone. She liked that idea. Anson had more experience on the sheets than Boot or Roscoe, or even the warden who had known only his fat wife. Anson plain knew more, and had that tall, lean body – must have been all them Indian maidens he coupled with when growing with the Apache. Maybe Apache women were better on the blanket than white women. What she knew for certain, it was sure pleasurable to be out, breathing clean, fresh, *free* air.

56

Marshal Leather Yates bounced beside her, trying to keep up. 'How many? From the past we got One-Eye Tim Brace and Wild Fletch Badger.'

'Sounds like a pair of first-class thinkers,' Pearl said.

'Good gun hands. We got you, and I assume, Roscoe.' He cleared his throat. 'I actually don't take part.'

'Then who needs you?'

'I organize the job.'

'That what you call it? Organize?'

'Logistics. I can get better information, being a town marshal and all. Besides, those boys will be enough to get it done. We don't need no more.'

'Roscoe has information. Plus, there's Hawkstone.'

'I wouldn't count on Hawkstone.'

'I *am* counting on him, for sentimental reasons. I want him with me.'

'He don't show much enthusiasm.'

'Then you do what it takes to enthuse him. Ain't that what it means by logistics? Ain't that organization?'

They reached the hotel and went inside.

The marshal said, 'We may have to force him. Find some way to make him want to go along. 'Course, maybe you can. . . .'

Pearl sweetened her voice, noticing the marshal liked to stare at her bodice. 'I'll do what I can, Marshal. Only, I ain't nothin' really but a woman. I don't know how much influence I'll have on him.'

'Oh, I think you do,' Marshal Leather Yates said.


With Pearl Harp in her room, Marshal Yates saw One-Eye Tim Brace and Wild Fletch Badger in the lobby of the Orndorff. He pressed them outside to the boardwalk. 'Let's find a saloon.'

'Won't be hard. This town's got one between every building,' One-Eye said. He stood short, about five-five. His left eye had been shot out during one of his many lifetime robberies; he kept his black plains Stetson pulled low on one side to shadow the cavity. His Remington pistol was tucked down his cartridge belt.

Wild Fletch Badger chomped a bite from a plug of chewing tobacco.

Past the Congress Hall Saloon, where town legislatures had once gathered when Tucson was capital of the Arizona Territory, was the Tucson Palace Saloon, an unpainted frontier watering hole, where clerks and interns and go-for runners tossed down mugs of beer and whiskey cut with some unknown substance. Next to that was where the two-dollar ladies hung out to ply their trade – the name usually with Gentlemen somewhere in it, though not many genuine gentlemen participated.

In the saloon, the three men took a corner table and ordered beer.

'When do we do this?' Wild Fletch Badger said. Fletch was raised by outlaws and had been a wild jasper his whole life – which was why Yates had chosen him. Skinny as a pole and just under six feet, he had a pinched buzzard face, dressed unclean and ragged, was quick to fight and quicker to shoot. He carried a Colt .45 on his right hip. His thinking came quick and shallow, and he took what he wanted without hesitation. His sudden movements usually showed thoughtless action.

The marshal said, 'Looks like we gotta wait for this Roscoe Dees fella, be in town tomorrow.'

Wild Fletch spat a gob of juice to the floor. 'How many we got so far?'

Yates glanced at them with his scarlet sunburned face, and at Fletch with disgust. He swallowed a slug of beer and wiped his mustache with the back of his pudgy hand. 'You two, Pearl Harp, her friend Roscoe – and maybe Anson Hawkstone.'

One Eye said, 'That's a lot of pieces cut from the pie – plus your handsome share.'

'It's a big pie,' the marshal said. 'According to the late Boot Hobson, it might go for fifty thousand or more.'

'Why do we need Hawkstone?'

'She wants him.' Marshal Yates grimaced in pain. His burned back hurt. His belly stung. Mostly, his swollen feet hurt from walking hot sand barefoot, scampering from shadow to shadow, now stinging and crushed in his new boots. Every movement made him catch his breath with pain. He wished to be in his room, the damned boots off, soaking his swollen feet in Epsom salts. Inside, his head burned with rage each time he heard Hawkstone's name.

Fletch drained his beer. 'I tell you one thing, I want the money that bastard got hid. At first, I just wanted a share on account of we got none of the bank robbery. Now, I want it all.' He spat on the floor again, adding to the peppered surface.

The marshal said, 'You'll have to kill him for it.'

'That ain't no problem for me.'

Marshal Yates leaned forwards with his elbows on the table. 'Wherever and whenever this hold-up happens, get this firm in your thinking: Hawkstone don't get no share 'cause he ain't to survive. I'm counting on you boys. You gun him down at the site and leave him for federal marshals to find. You shoot him dead.'

One-Eye leaned back in his chair. 'What if he won't come in with us on this?'

'The convict gal thinks she might convince him.'

'And what if she can't?'

'We go another way.'

'What other way?'

'We take something he cares about,' Marshal Leather Yates said. 'We go after that Apache princess, or the old woman.'

# TWELVE

In growing darkness, Anson Hawkstone rode his chestnut mare the back way into Tucson, from the Tombstone side. *Since greed and happiness never see each other, how should they ever become acquainted?* Maybe he wasn't dealing with much happiness, but there was sure enough greed to go around.

His arm still bothered him, but not so much any more. He rode along Main Street, past the Pennington Hotel at the corner of Pennington, and by the Hodge Hotel. Most stores and shops had closed. Houses put out frying meat cooking smells and sounds of subdued movement casting shadows against window lamp glow. The sounds of shouts and clinking glasses erupted from saloons south of the presidio. Close to Meyer Street he saw a light through the window of the Pima County Bank office. He walked the chestnut around to the back. A saddled bay mare stood tethered. The building sat isolated, the nearest structure fifty feet away – the Longfellow Copper Mining Company office. A hill of smooth boulders rose a hundred feet behind the buildings.

The back window of the bank showed a young man bent to a safe. He was dressed like a banker, with a brown suit and string tie. He wore no hat and his honey-brown hair shone in the light. Hawkstone aimed the chestnut to the edge of the hill and waited, blending into the dark cracks between rocks, and dismounted. He hadn't noticed a light on inside the mining office. When it blew out, the darkness drew his attention. A man shoved the back door of the office closed and locked it. He wore a bowler hat and had pork-chop whiskers on a cherub face; he was about fifty. Rubbing his hands together he walked straight for the back door of the bank. He knocked lightly. The inside of the bank went dark.

'Barron, you about ready?' the older man with the pork chops said. 'I'm headed for the hotel.'

The young man opened the door, and once out, he nodded, 'Jed.' He turned and locked the door.

'We set for dawn?' Jed asked.

The young man patted his suit jacket pockets, an aimless gesture. 'I think so.'

'Have time for a beer?'

'Ah, no, we have a poker game going at the Owl's Club.'

Jed chuckled. 'You and your Owl's Club for well-off bachelors – wish I was young and rich enough for all that poker and dancing and parties, and those gorgeous young women.'

'It isn't like that all the time.' He took the reins of the bay and walked beside Jed towards Main Street.

Hawkstone tied his chestnut's reins behind the bank where the bay had been, and followed twenty feet behind the two men. At the Hodge Hotel, Jed waved and the men parted. Barron Jacobs walked five feet more while Hawkstone closed the distance, then moved to mount the bay. Hawkstone stepped up behind him.

'Ease it right there, Barron.'

Barron stiffened and started to turn. 'Do I know you?'

'No.'

'Are you robbing me?'

'No. Don't turn around just yet. What kind of artillery you carrying?' He reached around and patted the suit coat. 'Slip the pistol out with your thumb and finger. Reach it behind you.'

Barron did what he was told. Hawkstone tucked the short barrel pistol under his cartridge belt.

They started walking. Jacobs in front leading the bay, said, 'Where are you taking me?'

'Right now, we're headed to where I tied my horse.'

When they reached the back of the bank, Hawkstone dragged out a bottle from his saddle-bag. With the bay tied next to the chestnut, he pointed Jacobs around to the backside of the rocks.

'What do you want?' the banker asked.

'Got some questions. Let's sit and get comfortable.' When they climbed five easy feet and sat on a pair of smooth, fairly flat boulders, Hawkstone said, 'Care for a snort?'

Barron Jacobs stared at Hawkstone. His face looked smooth, just over twenty showing shadows and lights, as slick and featureless as the boulders in little light. He looked at the bottle and shrugged, 'Sure, why not?' He took a good pull and swallowed with a sour face.

Hawkstone took his turn. 'Got the makings, Bull Durham and corn-skin paper.'

'Don't use it. I prefer a good cigar.'

'Ain't got none of them.'

They sat in silence while Hawkstone rolled his own. 'Tell me what happens at dawn.'

'No, I won't tell you about that.'

Hawkstone stuck the rolled cigarette between his lips and pulled his Colt .45 from the holster. 'Too much noise to shoot your ankle or elbow or knee cap – make you a cripple the rest of your life.' He tapped the barrel of the weapon on the banker's leg. 'But I can pistol whip you some. Now, you see the aiming sight there at the end of the barrel of this here six-gun? I ain't as mean as some fellas.

62

Some fellas sharpen that sight to a knife edge so's when they pistol whip another fella the cuts go deep and long. Still, this sight of mine can chew you up good enough. Be a long time 'fore you're handsome again.' He offered the bottle. 'Here, have another snort.' He struck a match and inhaled.

Barron Jacobs took the bottle with shaky fingers. 'We're loading the payroll,' he took another slug of whiskey, 'sending it to the mines on Tuesday, instead of the Wednesday stagecoach run.'

'All the way into New Mexico Territory? I was just up that way. It's a two-day trip.'

Jacobs nodded. 'Usually get to the horse change stage stop about midnight. Go on to the Longfellow mines by a different coach.'

'How many different drivers and coaches?'

Jacobs took another pull from the bottle. His tongue had loosened some. He acted proud of how smart he was. 'We have a contract with Longfellow Mining to deliver the payroll safely. The bank is weary of robberies so we need to take these measures.'

'How many taking it, Barron?'

'Four drivers, three coaches. Twice a month on the weeks between stagecoach runs. Leaving Tuesday at dawn, arrive at the mines late Wednesday or early Thursday.'

'And the stagecoach carries no money?'

'Just what passengers have on them.'

Hawkstone inhaled and blew smoke. He took a swallow from the bottle. He peered sideways at Jacobs: 'Now, you go to all this trouble, how do you fool stage robbers?'

'We used to put the payroll on the same stagecoach with executives headed back from a relaxing break – had four guards riding along with it. It even took a different route. But the route made no difference, and hold-up men found the way in New Mexico Territory and held it up anyway. A man in the mining office was telling them, for a share of the money. He's in prison now.'

Hawkstone took another pull on the bottle. 'What's his name, this man in prison?'

Jacobs shrugged. 'Roscoe something-or-other.'

'That's fascinatin', Barron, but I got another situation I want to toss at you. Suppose a fella was to come up to a stagecoach hold-up and all the polecats was dead? And suppose the bank money was just lying there with nobody around it? Now, this fella what come up on the others wants to do the right thing. He wants to turn the money over to the bank, but he figures he ought to get something for doing that, for doing the right thing.'

'Ten per cent,' Barron Jacobs said. 'The bank will give a ten per cent recovery reward.' He took the bottle and drank a swallow. He looked off towards the direction of the bank. 'You have bank money with you now?'

Hawkstone dropped the spent smoke and stomped his boot heel on it against the boulder. 'Nope, jest speculatin'. So, you can promise a fella would get ten per cent cash if he turned money back in that somebody else took from the bank?'

'Yes. But all of it returned, *then* we'd pay the reward.'

'You look young, Barron. You got enough clout to keep that promise? A lot of fellas make promises they just can't keep. They like to end a sentence with "I promise", only they ain't got the authority or sand to come through.'

'My family owns the bank. I'd have to run it past the board members, but I'm confident the bank would be happy to get any amount back.'

Hawkstone slid the Colt back in its holster. 'Confident, that's a nice civilized word. Now, all I got to figure is, are you and that board, men of honour.'

'Likely, as honorable as you.'

'Mebbe I ain't so honorable, but I keep my promises, and I finish what I set out to do, and I always ride for the brand. I don't want you running to the federal marshal about our little talk.'

'That was my next step, unless you kill me.'

'I will. You go right on with what happens at dawn, with no jabber to nobody else. From now until then, either one of my pards or me will have a bead on you. Any smell of the law or change in plan, you catch the first bullet.' Hawkstone stared at the banker. 'You got any doubt on my meaning?'

'No. The money is insured, but because of the robberies, the premiums have gotten out of control.' He rubbed his hands along his pant legs and squinted sideways. 'You're going after the payroll, aren't you?'

'I ain't no bank robber.'

'You could be lying.'

'Indeed, I could.'

'I can't see you clear and I don't even know your name.'

'We'll just keep it that way for now.'

# THIRTEEN

Tuesday, a while before sunrise, Anson Hawkstone met Black Feather, Burning Buffalo and Tommy Wolfinger in Tucson at the back of the boulder formation behind the bank and the mining office. They wore clothes taken during many Apache raids – farm clothes mostly, overalls, plain cotton shirts, high shoes, flat-top wide-brimmed hats, with large kerchiefs for their faces. Using cover from the rocks, they watched two men carry a strongbox to an open carriage parked between the bank and the mining office. The box was loaded on the back of the carriage and covered with a pink quilt and tied down. Jed, the pork-chop whiskered mining man, stood in front of the one-horse rig holding the reins to the hitched bay. A mature woman wearing a grey dress, her shoulders covered by a knitted black shawl, walked slowly from the mining office and climbed on to the small four-place carriage seat. She picked up the reins.

Barron Jacobs, in a blue banker suit, came from the bank and spoke to her. He looked around, directly at the boulders, and wrung his hands together. He put his hand on the woman's shoulder and moved his head back and forth for emphasis as he spoke – but he was too far away for Hawkstone to hear. The woman stared at the back of the bay, her pewter hair in a tight bun. She put on a short-brim plains hat and looked at Jacobs and nodded. Jed stepped aside, away from the horse. Two mounted men rode in with Winchesters, the rifle stock on their legs, pointed to the sky. With a rein slap on the bay the carriage moved on to Main and outside the Tucson city limits, the two armed men following.

Hawkstone and the three braves mounted and walked their horses until they were two blocks away, then set to a fast gallop. Hawkstone led because the banker had told him the way. With just one horse pulling the carriage at a walk and trot the going would be slow, along a little known trail from Tucson to the San Pedro river, then beside the river until north of Wharton City and the General Keambevs road, where the strongbox would be transferred to a faster buggy for the run towards New Mexico.

Hawkstone and the three braves rode hard, none

looking like Apache, hoofbeats pounding over desert scrub, galloping by arroyos and mesas, the kerchiefs still tied around their necks. With the carriage plodding along behind, they widened the distance, and rode straight for the San Pedro, figuring to hit the wagon close to the river bank. The sun rose slowly, burning off the misty dew. When he reckoned to be four or five miles ahead of the carriage, Hawkstone reined up to rest the horses – the pintos and the chestnut mare heaved from the effort as the men dismounted. They walked along slowly, holding the reins. Hawkstone took a pull from his canteen, while the others drew theirs. They poured water into their hats and stopped to let the horses drink. The three braves squatted and looked towards the river still out of sight. Hawkstone thought they appeared a little like farmers, but not by much, maybe immigrants.

Burning Buffalo had his long single braid tucked under the farmer hat. 'Do we kill?' he asked looking directly at Hawkstone. 'Do we take scalps?'

'No. We got to take out the two guards. I want you and Tommy upstream with your Winchesters. Use willows or cottonwoods or rocks for cover. Each of you hit one in the leg. Me and Black Feather will ride up and I'll try to outdraw the woman so she rests easy. I'm hoping the guards is just drovers looking for a little in-between eatin' money so they won't be looking on the job as a religion. Me and Black Feather will invite them to toss their hardware. They resist we'll have to wing 'em again.' He nodded to Burning Buffalo. 'You brought the big steel bar. We'll bust open the box right there on the wagon, move the cash to extra saddle bags I brought. The woman won't be able to load the guards in the wagon by herself so we'll have to help – with them trussed like rodeo doggies using our extra lariats. She can take the wagon on back to Tucson.'

Tommy Wolfinger stood tall and lithe and stretched. 'What you do with money?'

Hawkstone patted the chestnut's neck. The horses were no longer heaving for breath. He said, 'I don't trust the baby-faced banker or his board of directors. I figure to pull the reward right off the top. I'll bury the rest over Big Ears Kate and Billy Bob Crutch. Let Federal Marshal Casey Steel find it all. I might drop in the boots we took from Marshal Leather Yates, give Steel something to ponder.'

Black Feather chuckled. 'How we got boots was funny. I liked that.'

Hawkstone smiled with his blood brother.

But Tommy looked sceptical. He continued to stare at Hawkstone. 'What you do with reward money?'

Hawkstone checked the cinch on the chestnut. 'If the amount is close to fifty thousand, you each get a thousand. I'll take a thousand. The extra goes to the old woman, Saguaro Claw. She takes care of us and can use it.' He dropped the stirrup from the saddle horn and mounted. The three braves threw their legs over to sit in their saddles.

Black Feather squinted at Hawkstone. 'You will hold up the stagecoach with the outlaws anyway?'

'I may have to. We got to protect the band from harm, especially Hattie and the old woman.'

When the carriage approached the San Pedro River and was about to turn left upstream along the bank, Burning Buffalo and Tommy shot the two guards riding behind. Both bullets hit a calf. One guard fell from the saddle. The other jerked and bent enough to drop his Winchester. He immediately drew his pistol.

'Drop them or you're dead!' Hawkstone shouted from downstream willows.

The guard's pistol aimed at the willows, the rider still in

the saddle. The two braves emerged upstream from the wagon. Next to Hawkstone downstream, Black Feather shot the rider through his left shoulder. The force knocked him off his horse. He bounced against the strongbox and flipped to the river bank with grunts. The three braves closed in with drawn pistols. The standing guard dropped his Winchester. Hawkstone kept his Peacemaker on the woman and stepped to the carriage. She sat still as stone, staring at him without expression. The braves gathered pistols and rifles, removed cartridges and tossed them behind riverside rocks.

Hawkstone said, 'We ain't taking your weapons. You'll need them on down the trail.'

Black Feather already had his bowie knife. He made short work of the rope ties around the strong box. Burning Buffalo moved to the box with the steel bar.

The guard lying next to the carriage groaned. 'I'm bleedin' hard.'

'We'll get to you shortly,' Hawkstone said. He kept his aim at the woman, expecting her to make some kind of move.

The old brass lock stubbornly resisted, but in a few seconds of squeaks and grunts of effort the bar conquered it, and the lock snapped open with the sound of broken parts. Burning Buffalo studied the broken padlock while the others watched and waited. He tossed the brass into the river and pushed open the lid.

The strongbox was empty.

For a few seconds nobody moved. Hawkstone felt a tingle across his forehead, then the heat of anger. His eyes burned. He gritted his teeth, and his first thought was, somebody would die for this.

Burning Buffalo was the first to move. He dropped the steel bar, pulled his Remington from the cartridge belt and aimed it at the guard wounded in the shoulder lying by the carriage. 'We kill them all.'

'Wait.' It was the standing guard, shot in the leg.

With his left hand, Hawkstone grabbed a handful of the woman's dress close to her throat and dragged her from the seat. Her legs got tangled and she fell forward as he twisted her round and threw her to the ground on her back. He pushed his Colt against her forehead. 'In your last living seconds, where has the money gone?'

She looked like everybody's grandma, plump, thin vertical wrinkle lines above her upper lip, at the corners of her mouth, around her eyes – her pale blue eyes showed only a little fear, as if she had been there before and would accept what happened.

'Wait,' the guard said again. 'No need for killin'.'

With his Colt still pushed against the old woman's forehead, Hawkstone said to the guard, 'What's your name?'

'Perry Russell. You patch us up, and I'll tell you where the payroll went.'

'Other way around, Perry, where?' He pulled his Colt from the old woman.

Burning Buffalo and Tommy Wolfinger had their Remingtons aimed at the two guards, hammers cocked. They held their Winchesters loose in their left hand.

The San Pedro river splashed by them. Insects hovered above the smooth surface, some snatched by trout; patchy tree shade shielded the sun.

Perry Russell limped to the back of the wagon and grabbed it for support. He wore a Montana peak hat and was dressed in drover clothes. His thin, weathered face carried the texture and tone of well-worn rawhide. He belonged with a trail herd pushing along the Chisolm. He looked directly at Hawkstone's kerchief-wrapped face.

'They runnin' the cash pony-express style – a rider lit out

after us headed north at full gallop for Fort Grant, with crammed extra saddle-bags. He changes horses and rides by Wharton City to the General's route – another horse change and a new rider where Bonito Creek joins the Rio Gila – that rider heads east towards New Mexico Territory. Another new rider changes mounts close to Steeple Rock and rides full on to Fort Webster. Then another new fella takes the saddle-bags up to the mines.' Perry slumped against the wagon out of breath.

Hawkstone spun to Black Feather who had already holstered his weapon and was walking to his pinto. 'Your mount is fastest.' He turned back to Perry Russell. 'How come you know this?'

Russell coughed, and looked hard at his bleeding leg. 'I was hired to be that new rider waitin' with two fellas bringing a fresh horse at Bonito Creek, us waitin' by the connection with the Rio Gila for them saddle-bags. When I was a young'un I used to ride the Express, reason the Longfellow hired me. But they decided I was too old for such bouncin' around energy, and told me to ride guard on this here carriage.' He grimaced in pain. 'I got to get somethin' wrapped around this leg.' He looked towards the river. 'Life drivin' cattle is sure easier than this.'

Hawkstone ignored him and the grandma and turned back to Black Feather, who had hold of his pinto's reins. 'Bonito Creek – two riders, three horses, another comin'.'

The words were unnecessary. Black Feather, the best tracker in the territories, had already swung into the saddle and was racing off at a full gallop even before his farmer shoes slipped into the stirrups.

# FOURTEEN

In the darkness of the second night Hawkstone saw Black Feather waiting by the fork where Bonito Creek joined the Rio Gila river. Black Feather crouched the Apache way, a bottle in his hand, dressed again in his buckskin, no kerchief.

First off, Hawkstone said, 'You kill them?'

Black Feather handed Hawkstone the bottle to share. 'No need. They expected a friendly rider. Now they are tied and blindfolded, back in that strand of cottonwoods. I never would have caught him, but the rider had supper at Fort Grant, and three drinks. He rode a fresh horse, but the delay was enough. What about the carriage?'

Hawkstone, Burning Buffalo and Tommy Wolfinger stepped wearily down and crouched with Black Feather to share the whiskey. The braves looked as worn and beaten as Hawkstone felt. He passed around Bull Durham and cornskin paper, except for Tommy, and blinked his tired, burning eyes. 'We patched the boys and got them in the carriage. Perry Russell was well enough to drive. The woman rode shotgun. When they get back to Tucson the word will go out, by rider or wire, or both. They'll come looking now.'

'If they can find us.' Black Feather took his pull from the bottle and lit the cigarette. 'The saddle-bags come up short.'

Hawkstone took the bottle. 'How short?'

'They got forty-eight thousand, not fifty.'

'So ten per cent reward money is forty-eight hundred. I'll take the short straw on account of I got my ten thousand from the Mineral City square dance. What you want to do with the four men?'

Burning Buffalo removed his hat so the long single braid dropped free. He took a match light from Hawkstone and said, 'Take their horses – and the remount.'

Black Feather nodded. 'They're trussed good. Might work off the blindfolds; if they crawl their way out somebody will find them. They will not need horses. There is a fine-looking appaloosa I want. My pinto is worn ragged.'

Tommy Wolfinger took his pull from the bottle and turned to Hawkstone. 'Who gets the extra horse? We take one each, who gets the fifth?'

'I'll give mine and the extra to Hattie. She can look after them for a spell.'

Tommy's lips tightened. 'You give her them for payment to her bed?'

Hawkstone stood and inhaled and blew his smoke. 'This ain't the time or place. You and Burning Buffalo can tangle belt buckles over her later when we got this money thing cleared up. The copper mine people are already coming. The payroll was supposed to be there, and it ain't. Them or the bank will send regulators to gun us down. They'll be backtracking the stops and will find those four jaspers soon enough. We ain't even got time to rest 'til we're well clear of this place and Black Feather has made our trail disappear. We'll water and feed the animals and take our little remuda west, home. We got to alter the brands on the new mounts in case copper men get that far. We got to leave, *now.*'

Tommy drained the last of the whiskey and squinted. 'Go back to do what?'

Hawkstone smiled. 'Go back to being cowboys and

Indians.' He winked at them. *'If a man could have half his wishes, he'd double his troubles.'*

Black Feather chuckled. 'Another Franklin.'

The braves nodded with smiles, then mounted.

Though the old woman did not smile, her gnarled, seasoned mahogany face showed her satisfaction having the men of her small tribe safely returned. She had rock goat jerky and cactus berries and real coffee for them.

In the wickiup, after Hawkstone returned from the burned house, having used the shovel again, he slept most of the evening and through the night. He woke in the stir of daylight with slight pain along his arm, but felt refreshed. He smelled mesquite and juniper, and cottonwood fire smoke that in the still morning wafted grey and straight up, and mushroomed, spreading and extending in shrouds around tepees and wickiups, and hung still, only shifting when broken by village life moving around. He caught the scent of brewing coffee. He rubbed sleep from his eyes, watching through the open doorway.

Mongrel dogs stretched, front paws straight out, rump in the air, then trotted about sniffing the ground as they went. Pigs snorted as they hunted for scraps of food. Chickens pecked at old eating sites. A horse whinnied for company. Crows that perched in cottonwood and willow branches cawed to announce life shifting on the village ground below. Waking humans stirred inside tepees and wickiups, coughing and clearing their throats. Little children stayed inside, it being too early and the chill too penetrating for them to run outside in play just yet. Groups of boys just past ten took bows and arrows for a morning hunt. Girls helped begin the first meal next to their mothers.

He saw the old woman bent outside at the campfire with Hattie Deep Water. Apache ate roasted prairie dog or venison or other available game for breakfast, but the old woman knew Hawkstone was partial to fried eggs. She scrambled four of them in melted bacon grease using the old stolen white man frying pan and silver spoon.

Outside the wickiup, Hawkstone strapped on his cartridge belt and stretched. The village exhaled the stir of life and comfort. It was his village, his home. And these were his people. He was aware of Hattie watching him, her almond eyes dancing. Volcano, the vicious part-dog, lay just beyond the village along the first row of cottonwood trees, watching her. He growled when he saw Hawkstone. Hattie stood and hugged Hawkstone, her young body tight against him, arms around his neck, her cheek against his. Silently, she moved back to the fire. She handed him a cup of coffee. When she bent again she yanked the frying pan from the old woman.

'Let me.' She said. 'I must grow used to this.' Her buckskin skirt barely reached her calf moccasins and showed a flash of slim bare leg.

The old woman allowed her to take the pan, and basted the rabbit that sizzled on a limb spit over the flame.

'Behave yourself, girl,' Hawkstone said. She reminded him of a young deer, lithe, lean, graceful and quick. Her long, shiny black hair framed her flawless face, and those dark, almond eyes melted any man they aimed at. And didn't she know it.

She held the pan close to the fire, and slid the spoon back and forth through the eggs. 'You have already given me two of the horses you need.'

The old woman hissed at her. 'Foolish, silly girl.'

Hawkstone took the pan and spoon and sat on a log. The old woman handed him a wooden plate. He slid the eggs to the plate and began to eat with the silver spoon. He and the old woman locked eyes.

'Keep her close,' he said. 'Men may come looking.'

The old woman nodded. 'You were later than the others.'

Hawkstone spooned in the eggs and they tasted good. He sipped coffee. 'I had something to bury at the burned shack.'

'I ride out there,' Hattie said. 'Today, I will ride one of the marriage horses you brought, out to the burned shack then to the Rio Gila where I swim and bathe. Come with me, Anson.'

'I have to meet some fellas in Wharton City.' He pointed a finger at Hattie. 'I don't want you riding too far from the village. Stay close a few days, help out.'

She wrinkled her nose. 'Why? I do what I please. I ride where I want. Volcano always protects me. He will until I am yours. Then you will protect me.'

He ate the last of the eggs. 'Think about Burning Buffalo and Tommy Wolfinger, and which you will choose. They are the men for you. Choose one.'

'I have already chosen. You need a young woman to look after you in your ancient creaky days and nights.'

The old woman hissed at her again. 'Stop this foolish little girl talk. Hawkstone will leave again soon.'

Hattie shivered. Her brow wrinkled. She turned to stare at Hawkstone. Then she relaxed and shrugged. 'When he leaves, I will go with him.'

Black Feather joined them and crouched by the campfire. 'White man's ways make me crave coffee,' he said.

The old woman had just taken a bite of rabbit. She poured and handed him a full cup. 'No sugar.'

Black Feather shrugged and sipped coffee. 'With your new wealth, old woman, you can afford sugar.' He looked at Hawkstone. 'You have meeting with the gang today.'

Hawkstone sucked his tongue against his teeth and set the plate aside and pulled his Bull Durham pouch to start the makings for a smoke. He handed the pouch and paper to Black Feather. The old woman and Hattie ate hot cooked rabbit.

'I got to decide,' Hawkstone said.

Black Feather lit his cigarette. 'I will ride with you.'

The old woman glared at Black Feather. 'You eat rabbit.'

Black Feather grimaced, his face still wrinkled with sleep. 'I am not hungry.'

'You eat rabbit,' the old woman snapped. 'No backtalk, pup. You eat rabbit, then you smoke and drink coffee and talk with Hawkstone.'

Black Feather chuckled. He grinned at Hawkstone while he pulled a strip of rabbit. 'No Franklin this morning about grouchy old women?'

'Ah,' Hawkstone said. '*You can't pluck roses without thorns, and you can't enjoy a woman without the danger of horns.*' He pointed at Black Feather. 'Eat your rabbit.'

# FIFTEEN

*Many foxes grow grey, not many grow good.*

Hawkstone met them in a private room that Vicki Verona had arranged on the ground floor towards the back of the Gentlemen Kingdom, house of pleasure. The room was hung with red and green velvet for curtains, there was a dresser with bottles of liquor and glasses, and it was dominated by a long table surrounded by seven fancy, swirl-purple, velvet armchairs. Hawkstone reckoned the room looked classier than its occupants. He entered ready, his Colt Peacemaker .45 well oiled, with every cylinder filled – no empty for the hammer. The rawhide thong was off.

As soon as he was inside, Pearl Harp pushed into his arms. On tip-toe she gave him a long, wet kiss. 'Parts of you I miss something terrible, Anson,' she whispered. Her tiny body felt firm and well shaped against him. She wore a bright green, scoop neck dress – brown eyes soft, her small face painted just enough to look somewhat attractive.

Marshal Leather Yates said, 'Nobody will listen in and we won't be disturbed.' He avoided looking directly at Hawkstone.

Wild Fletch Badger added tobacco spit to the pepper-stained, bare wooden floor.

With Pearl still clinging on his arm, Hawkstone took in those around him. One-Eye Tim Brace had put on a clean shirt. His hat still hung low in front to shadow the empty eye socket. Wild Fletch Badger hadn't bothered to clean up. His pinched buzzard face worked around the plug of tobacco while he stared at Hawkstone through beady eyes full of hate. Marshal Yates still had a sunburn flush to his face. He stood behind the chair at the head of the table, his chubby hands on the back taking possession of it. Pearl Harp led Hawkstone around the table to a chair next to her along the side. After they sat, she placed his left hand on her lap. Across from them was a man he didn't know.

Pearl bowed to the man. 'Anson Hawkstone, meet Roscoe Dees. He is our information man.'

'And outlaw informer, I hear,' Hawkstone said.

One Eye Tim Brace and Wild Fletch Badger flanked Dees at the table. Badger looked around for a place to spit, turned his head and let fly to the floor.

Pearl slapped the table. 'Find a container, you pig, or sit outside. Even better, swallow!'

Badger blinked at her, then narrowed his eyes and tightened his lips. 'You don't talk to me like that, prison whore.' The words were mumbled because his mouth was full.

Marshal Leather Yates slid a whiskey glass down the table to him. 'Use that.'

Hawkstone rested his right hand on the Colt walnut grip. He lined them up in order as to who he would shoot first if he had to. Across the table was a good pair to start with, then Marshal Yates for sure.

Roscoe Dees still glared at Hawkstone. 'Mister, I do not inform outlaws.'

'Not lately,' Hawkstone said. 'You been locked up.'

Marshal Yates cleared his throat as if to demand attention. 'Why don't we have Roscoe there tell us what he knows about the Pima County Branch bank and their payroll for Longfellow Copper Mining? Go ahead, Roscoe.'

Dees looked mousy and devious at the same time. He wore a grey wool suit and no hat, his spider-web, mud-hole-tainted hair parted just above his left ear. His brown eyes stared through magnified spectacles looking like dirty quarters. His teeth were brown-yellow bad, with a gap instead of one eyetooth. He had a long, pointed nose and a worm mouth, with more spider web across his upper lip. His appearance might have conjured up many impressions, but not one of them was trust. He shifted uncomfortably, receiving stares from everyone else in the room, who waited to listen.

He stared at the table top in front of him, shot a glance at Hawkstone, and said, 'I wonder if I might have a glass of water.'

Yates said, 'Later, clerk. Start talking.'

Roscoe Dees cleared his throat. 'I still have a friend at the bank. But you must understand they keep their activity guarded in secrecy these days. Something happened in the last day or two, but nobody is talking. It is one secret among many, but it is big. They used to send the payroll with the executives – the company officers, along another route to the way station outside Fort Webster. Guards rode out of sight, flanking the coach. When I went to prison they stopped that, and began sending other wagons – prairie schooners, buckboards, carriages – and they sent them on the day before, Tuesday instead of Wednesday. Today is Thursday, so it would have been next week.'

Marshal Yates said, 'We don't give a hoot in hell how they used to do it, we want to know how they do it next week. How are they moving the payroll?'

'That's what I'm trying to tell you. It will be on the stage-coach with the copper company vice-president, Mr Brennan, and three bank officers next Wednesday, their usual schedule. Mr Jacobs thinks nobody will expect that. Four guards will be riding out of sight. I don't know where they will make their first horse change, likely somewhere along the General Keambevs route. They may have a way station there. I only know about the station ten miles before Fort Webster in New Mexico Territory.'

Marshal Yates took a slug from his whiskey glass. Wild Fletch Badger spat brown into his glass. One-Eye Tim Brace pulled his hat brim lower. Pearl Harp looked to her right. Hawkstone sat with his hand on Pearl's lap. His palm gripped the outline of her leg. He liked the slim, firm feel of the dress.

After a silence, Yates said, 'We hit the stagecoach at Steeple Rock.' He nodded to Fletch. 'You and One-Eye Tim backshoot the guards soon as they get on the General's route. Pearl, Hawkstone and Roscoe will dog the stagecoach 'til you boys catch up, then you take it together. You'll have to kill the shotgun and mebbe the driver. The important men inside I leave to you. If they got to go, they got to go.'

Roscoe Dees shook his head, 'Oh, no, no, no. I cannot

take part. I am not a man for hold-ups – no, sir, not me.'

Yates leaned forward over his glass. 'You mean, not until now.'

Pearl put her elbows on the table. 'That's quite a blood bath, Marshal. It ain't needed.'

'I say what's needed,' the marshal said.

Roscoe gaped across the table at Pearl. 'I did what you wanted. I found the information.' He glanced at Hawkstone. 'My dear, I see your affection has moved off in another direction. I am on my way to Santa Fe.'

'Like hell,' the marshal said.

'Like any way my horse will take me, Marshal. I will not take part in any murdering thievery. I already tasted prison life and I have no intention of repeating the experience.'

Marshal Yates said, 'Fletch, take the weasel outside and shoot him. Get him away from town.'

Pearl said, 'Anson?'

Hawkstone smelled panic in the room. He watched Fletch stand with a hand on Roscoe's collar. Hawkstone pushed his chair and stepped back, the .45 in his hand pointed at Wild Fletch Badger. 'Sit down or you're dead.' He kept his eyes on the buzzard face but talked to the marshal. 'Yates, if the skunk doesn't sit, you're dead too.'

'You can't shoot in two directions, Hawkstone,' the marshal said.

'I can shoot too,' said Pearl. She had her pistol on the table aimed at the marshal's puffed chest. 'I got the other direction, Anson, go ahead and shoot the bastard.'

Fletch Badger released the collar and quickly sat, his hatred staring at Hawkstone.

One-Eye Tim Brace had dropped his right hand from the table.

Hawkstone swung his aim, saying 'You come up with anything in your hand, and you're the first to go.'

The hand came up empty.

Marshal Yates held out his palms. 'All right, let's hold on here. We supposed to be planning something makes us all rich.' His pork-chop whiskers jiggled with his talking jowls. 'Settle down, folks, jest ease up. Now, Anson you put that hogleg away. Pearl, you just settle yourself. We're business associates here. We ain't got to love each other, but we got a job to do. We got to work together.'

Hawkstone and Pearl did not move.

Hawkstone ignored the marshal. 'Roscoe, you don't know cow milk from whitewash. Get yourself on out of here. Find your horse and ride for Santa Fe. You might think about moving farther along. Don't ever come back here. You already know better than to talk about this.'

Roscoe bowed as he slid back the chair, his lips pursed. 'What about my five hundred dollars?'

'You got a life,' Hawkstone said, 'don't git greedy.'

Roscoe squinted as if he was about to cry. 'I was *promised.*' He waited. He sighed and moved out of the room.

'And I'm another,' Hawkstone said.

Yates yanked his gaze from the retreating banker and stared at Hawkstone. 'What about you?'

'Another that won't be with you.'

Pearl stood, her pistol still on Yates. 'Anson? What are you saying?'

Marshal Yates looked around the table. He nodded. 'We'll change your mind.'

'Don't try,' Hawkstone said.

Yates looked at Pearl.

Pearl said, 'Anson, let's go to my hotel and talk about this. Maybe *I* can change your mind.'

# SIXTEEN

As morning brightened Pearl's hotel room, Anson Hawkstone sat on the edge of the bed pulling on his boots.

Pearl, propped up on her pillow, smoked a cigarette, one of the ready-mades from South Carolina she kept in a silver case. 'I need you with us, Anson.' She wore only a white chemise, looking perky with a young girl shape. Her experienced morning face showed different from perky.

Once dressed, he reached for his cartridge belt and swung it around his hips. He turned to her. 'Walk away from this, Pearl. It carries a bad smell beginning to end.'

'You didn't enjoy yourself during the night?'

'I did. I conjured up some fine memories, past and present.'

'But you ain't changed your mind – memories weren't good enough for you to bend to me?'

'Nope.'

'What if I promised more of the same until the stage-coach is done? And after?'

He looked around the room for his Stetson. 'I'd be tempted, but not enough. And what if there ain't no payroll on that stagecoach?'

'Roscoe says there will be.'

Hawkstone sat back on the edge of the bed and caressed her shoulders and breasts. He'd sure miss her. 'You believe Roscoe?'

Pearl's thin face scrunched up. 'What do you know, Anson?'

He kissed her forehead. 'You're the only outlaw I care about. It ain't no good, Pearl. I don't want you part of it. Ride on north to your folks and children.'

Pearl squashed the cigarette butt in a whiskey glass on the walnut night stand. She put her hand on the back of his neck. 'You got to come, Anson. If I can't convince you, the marshal will find another way.'

'He can try. I'll shoot him down when he does. I already reckon he killed Big Ears Kate and Billy Bob Crutch. I buried evidence it was him for Casey Steel. The town marshal ain't gonna live much longer, girl, and you got to get out of this.'

She kissed him, and he enjoyed the kiss while he caressed her. He hoped she'd soon be gone to other parts, and for a long time – and he hoped it would be soon, like tomorrow at the latest. He thought about telling her Roscoe didn't know the payroll had been sent, not only the day before schedule, but the week before. There would be no payroll for their hold-up. But he realized she'd just go running to Yates with the information, and the boys would come gunning for him, or worse, tell Federal Marshal Casey Steel that Hawkstone had the payroll money, along with his ten thousand from the Mineral City robbery three years before.

'Come back to bed, Anson,' she whispered. 'I want more of you.'

He stood again and sighed deeply. 'Listen to what I say, Pearl. I wish I could tell you more, but I can't. Get yourself gone. Promise me.'

'I'll think about it. You think about how you'll miss me. I know you'll miss me.'

At the door, he said, 'Damned if I won't. *Adios*, little girl.'

A mile from the small village, Hawkstone rode easy, letting the chestnut walk, her legs still wet from crossing the Rio

Gila where Disappointment Creek forked into it. He rode along the creek letting the chestnut pick her way. Then a pony galloping came splashing out of the Rio Gila and slowed up behind him. He had expected Black Feather sooner, just outside the whorehouse. The appaloosa heaved and shook his head as it trotted alongside. His antics caused the chestnut to snort and toss her head.

'A long fast ride?' Hawkstone said.

Black Feather reached back for his canteen and took a long swallow. 'Most fifty miles roundabout.' He leaned forwards and patted the appaloosa's neck. 'Easy, old timer.'

Hawkstone then knew. 'You followed Roscoe Dees. He was headed for Santa Fe.'

'That his name? I see him come from meeting. I follow south, not north towards Santa Fe.'

Hawkstone studied his tired-looking blood brother. 'He rode to Tucson, to the bank.'

'And went inside the bank,' Black Feather said.

'He likely found his five hundred dollars, the back-biting snake.'

Black Feather said, 'I know nothing about that. Does he tell the people at the bank about the hold-up?'

'And when and where it will take place.' Hawkstone pulled cigarette makings from his vest pocket as the chestnut walked along. The appaloosa had settled to the pace. 'I better tell them. There'll be more than four guards now – might even be regulators from the mines.'

They remained silent; their mounts clomped along, picking their way along the creek, around willows and rocks and past gnarled trunk junipers. In some places they could not see the creek because of the size of the boulders. The way was shadowy, with the setting sun hiding behind trees. Already Hawkstone smelled smoky fires and roasting desert rock goat flanks from the village. Hunting had gone well, with plenty to eat. Burning Buffalo would have seen there was plenty for the old woman and Hattie Smooth Water – the maiden princess owned the brave's heart. After handing the makings across to Black Feather, Hawkstone lit and drew burning Bull Durham into his lungs. His belly told him roasting goat smelled tasty.

When Black Feather was smoking, he said, 'Do you ride with the stagecoach hold-up?'

'I told them, no.'

Black Feather twisted to frown at him. 'You should not have told them.'

'I ain't going.'

'Then do not go, but say nothing. Let them think you are with them.'

'I want them to know.'

Black Feather stared forward blowing smoke. 'Now they must convince you. How do you think they will do that?'

'We have to be ready for them.'

'Not all of us can be ready.'

'We'll keep close, watch over each other. If they come, we'll know.'

'Perhaps,' Black Feather said.

They rode closer to the village, seeing smoke now, columns that rose and spun away with the evening breeze. Roasting goat aroma dominated. Dogs caught the riders' scent and began to bark until they became familiar. The dogs ran back and forth, acted excited, expecting scraps. Ahead, Hawkstone saw the first tepee of the village.

He said, 'Tomorrow, I go look at the first stop where they change horses. I never knew of such a stop. I want to see who is there – how many.'

'I will be with you,' Black Feather said. 'Where will the hold-up be?'

'Steeple Rock. Way I figure it, if a wire is sent to the

mines from the bank, regulators might already be riding for the New Mexico trail, ready to jump us outlaws. They might even put on extra guards. Bad business, my brother. The only hold-up outlaw I care about is Pearl Harp. I don't want her there. The rest can get shot up ten ways from Sunday.'

Black Feather watched the smoke columns. 'You and the mature woman with the young girl body shared a pillow, yes?'

'I did.'

Black Feather nodded, 'You are belly empty of food and head empty of sleep, but full of woman now.'

'I am.'

'It is good,' Black Feather said. 'Perhaps I will find a girl to share my tepee tonight.'

'I recommend it.'

'No Franklin for me in my quest?'

Hawkstone said, '*A house without a woman and fireplace is like a body without soul or spirit.*'

# SEVENTEEN

The day after the meeting, Wharton City Marshal Leather Yates took One Eye Tim Brace and Wild Fletch Badger on a ride towards the Apache village. They had spent the morning waiting and watching when they saw Anson Hawkstone and his Apache pard ride out, headed who knew where? Now, as the sun approached noon, they lay on their bellies on a bluff watching the old woman's wickiup, highly interested in the movements of the young Apache princess, known as Hattie Smooth Water. Young braves of the village had gone hunting for rock desert goats. Noisy children bounced around mothers and grandmothers. Mongrel dogs wrestled and snarled at each other. Hattie helped the old woman clean up after breakfast. They spoke low together, saying things they had saved until after the men left, most words too far to hear. From snatches of talk Marshal Yates did hear, Hattie was concerned over Hawkstone leaving the village for good. The old woman snapped at her to be silent, and stop giving pains in the head with her chatter. The girl would couple with whatever brave gave the old woman the most horses.

About an hour after noon, Hattie Smooth Water mounted an appaloosa filly and rode out of the village, headed for Hawkstone's burned-down shack. The half-dog trotted alongside. Staying far enough back so as not to be seen, the marshal and his boys followed.

Marshal Leather Yates's skin still burned enough that riding was uncomfortable.

One Eye Tim Brace trotted his mount beside the marshal. 'Marshal, you figure holding the girl will make Hawkstone throw in with us?'

Yates stared ahead. 'Plus fringes. He ain't gettin' her back as pure as he left her.'

On the other side of Yates, Wild Fletch Badger spat a brown glob into the dust and said, 'I want some of that, too.'

'We all do,' Yates said. 'You boys jes' remember the law goes first.'

The three slowed their mounts to a walk, keeping pace with the Apache girl shimmering ahead on the horizon.

One Eye said, 'I dunno, Marshal. We got no idea how the outlaw will react when we tell him about the girl, and how he better throw in with us on the stagecoach hold-up. He's liable to jes' start shootin'.'

'Then we gun him down before the hold-up,' Marshal Yates said. 'Thing is, I want his body there by the coach, him dead along with all them other folks he shot down.' He took his time looking from one to the other. 'Him dead with his Chiricahua pards evidence all around – a coupla arrows, mebbe stuck in a stagecoach passenger – mebbe a tomahawk split down a skull, mebbe a scalp taken. No witnesses to say it went different.'

Wild Fletch spit then sat straight in his saddle, 'We killin' them all, even them high up important men inside the stagecoach? We taking a scalp?'

'You can do it, Fletch. I got confidence in you. No witnesses means no witnesses.'

'Even Pearl Harp?'

Yates turned to stare at Wild Fletch. 'How big a split you want? Five ways, four ways, or three ways?'

One Eye said, 'I figured to get me some of that Pearl Harp.'

'You got five days,' the marshal said. 'You can catch her alone someplace and help yourself. Her body has to go over a cliff someplace. It wouldn't look good having her there in the slaughter of attack by Hawkstone and his crazy murderin' Apache brothers.'

One Eye shook his head, pulling his hat against the wind low over the cavity. 'I think she's a lot meaner than she looks. She's liable to shoot my private parts right off'n me 'fore I get a chance at any sugar.'

'Then forget her,' Yates said. 'Concentrate on what's ahead of us.'

'Yeah,' Wild Fletch said, as he spat.

'Yeah,' One Eye said, squinting at the girl towards the horizon in front of him.

They rode in silence for a spell, following the girl

towards the burned-down shack.

Wild Fletch said, 'How come an Apache attack on the stagecoach?'

The marshal wriggled in the saddle to relieve some of the sunburn pain. 'So I can alert the cavalry over there at Fort Grant. So them soldier boys ride in to punish the murderin' hostiles and destroy their village – where I think Hawkstone has that ten thousand bank money hidden.'

'I want that money,' Wild Fletch said.

Yates bobbed his head in the same movement as his horse. 'I know you do,' he said.

His feet squeezed into his boots was what hurt most. Where he sat in the saddle came next. But he figured that when the time came he'd have no trouble functioning as a man, especially with a sweet morsel like the princess, and with the boys holding her. He had to figure where they'd hide her when they sent the note to Hawkstone tied to her horse – either ride with them against the stagecoach, or the princess would die. He thought of Rocky Face Fiona at the Way Out Saloon. A shed sat in back, just beyond shouting distance from the outhouse. The girl might be tied up in there. Fiona owed the marshal, who allowed her to sell her fiery concoction as whiskey without tax and permitted him some of her bony, scraggy, personal sugar on occasion. One more small favour would be just another slice off the loaf – hardly noticed.

Wild Fletch broke the silence spitting a big gob that emptied his mouth. 'Something you got to figure, Marshal. While me and Tim here is off taking care of the guards, only Hawkstone and Pearl will dog the stagecoach. Suppose they don't wanna wait until we get there? They could warn them important minin' men inside, be layin' in wait for us.'

'That won't happen.'

'How come not?' One Eye asked.

'Because I'll be there with them. I'm riding along on this one, boys. I'll be keeping a close look-see on them two, plus the stagecoach. Everything will be ready when you boys show with your Apache gear.'

'They'd recognize you, Marshal. The way you sit a horse, they'd know for sure it was you, a lawman from Wharton City.'

The marshal smiled as he saw the charred shack skeleton ahead. 'Not if none of them is around to talk.'

They shot the dog first. After Hattie Smooth Water removed her clothes and waded into the Rio Gila, Yates and the boys had been watching and now closed the distance. As soon as they dismounted, the dog attacked the fattest and most aggressive of them. The dog came running fast between willows from the edge of the water, running low with a growl in its throat. One Eye Tim Brace drew his Colt and shot the dog through the side. The force was enough to knock the animal off his feet, cause him to slide sideways five steps. He came back up, legs still running. With his hands shaking in fear, Yates turned back to mount his horse, get up and away from the attacking animal, but he couldn't get his fat leg high enough, fast enough. His boot jerked on the edge then slipped down from the stirrup. Even wounded, the dog got a fang grip on the back of the marshal's leg before One Eye tore out the animal's belly with another shot.

Hattie Smooth Water screamed and started swimming fast for the opposite bank.

Yates shook the dog away and tried to see the wound by twisting around his ample girth. 'Fletch!'

Marshal Yates watched the river while he rubbed the back of his leg. Wild Fletch Badger dropped his gunbelt, and hopping to get one boot off, splashed into the river

91

after the girl. One Eye Tim Brace took enough time to get both his boots off. He unfastened his cartridge belt, then ran along the bank downriver almost out of sight before he went in and swam for the opposite shore. Hattie made it across, but her feet and hands kept slipping on the muddy bank until she dug her heels in. Then she ran naked between tree trunks, downriver until she saw One Eye almost across ahead of her. She turned back to see Wild Fletch Badger climb the bank and remove his other boot. She was caught between them.

Wild Fletch held out his hands, breathing quickly. 'Now, come along, sweetie. Ain't nobody gonna hurt you. You give us what we want; you go along on your way, nobody to bother you no more.'

Yates watched as Hattie picked up a tree limb the size of her arm. She leaned her back against a willow and looked first left, then right. She held the limb with both hands. Her body glistened. The long raven hair half covered her face and hung to her cute butt. Her lovely wet face scrunched in terror and determination. She raised and lowered the limb and raised it again to her shoulder. With a head movement she tossed her hair behind her shoulder. She took a step away from the willow. She waited for them. No words spoken, none needed.

Yates, across the river, pulled his Colt. He thought to wound her, maybe slow her thinking down some, make it easier for the boys to grab her and bring her back across to him. After the fear of the attacking dog, he now looked at that lithe naked body with lust, eager to touch her. He licked his lips while the boys closed in. He felt heat in familiar areas. He decided not to shoot – he'd likely kill her.

Hattie Smooth Water managed to strike One Eye Tim Brace – who didn't see so well with that cavity – once across the head. She swung for Wild Fletch, but he quickly moved in and grabbed the branch with a backhand to her face.

And they had her.

Marshal Leather Yates tried to shut out the guttural animal grunts of the two men on the mud in tree shadow while he pulled his clothes from the saddle. He didn't want to dress. He wanted more. And more. He didn't want those swine to crawl over her, slapping and fist punching away her whimpers. One Eye looked grotesque with his black dirty cavity where an eye was supposed to be. The mean Wild Fletch Badger liked to slap and hit and squeeze and hurt, making her cry out while he did his business. She was so sweet and innocent, and deserved the marshal's gentle kind of loving. He had been the first with her, and that had to give her a memory, as honeyed as his – maybe not a nightmare. He even thought about shooting them and taking her away with him. But that made no sense. They had to get the stagecoach. He held his clothes, not yet stepping into his pants. He would order them off her and wash her clean and take her to another place where he'd enjoy her again. They both kept slapping her, telling her to shut up.

And then Wild Fletch Badger hit her too hard.

And when her whimpers stopped, the boys stood and stared at her, wearing their wet shirts and vests and kerchiefs – only their pants and boots removed. They looked at each other, then at her, then sheepishly at the marshal when he put on his pants and joined them.

One Eye said, 'We was too rough with her.'

'You're animals,' Yates said. She lay so still, her mouth slack, eyes staring without seeing, black hair a nest around her face, beautiful body bleeding along her legs, and still, so still. 'You belong with whores,' he said, 'you should lie with dogs.'

'Mebbe so, Marshal,' Wild Fletch said, looking at the

body as if the words didn't matter to him. 'She wasn't very strong – thought she might hold up better, not be so fragile – thought she might last longer than she did. You're right, whores is tougher, they're used to rough treatment so they got more stamina.' He shrugged, then sighed, and turned to the marshal with a blank expression. 'So, what we gonna do now?'

Marshal Yates stiffened and frowned, turning his pork-chop whiskers left and right. 'What was that?'

One Eye and Wild Fletch looked around them. One Eye said, 'I didn't hear nothin'.'

'Feet running on the mud,' the marshal said. 'Brush rustlin'. I think mebbe somebody saw us, been watching.'

The three walked along the bank. One Eye said, 'That dog set a warp in you, Marshal. There ain't nobody.'

Yates shrugged. He looked back to the girl, swept his gaze up and down the river, and exhaled with a shudder. Sweet, innocent, but gone – he had to get back to the task at hand. That was real.

He said, 'Push her in the river. She'll float on down to the Colorado and likely be in Mexico 'fore anyone finds her. Throw the dog in, too. We'll take her clothes to the shack behind the Way Out Saloon; leave them there for Hawkstone and his murderin' Apache to find. I got the note already writ. Catch her appaloosa and we'll cut the pony loose at the village, give Hawkstone some reading material.'

One Eye said, 'She whispered something jest before she went, kept saying it with her grunts while we done her. She said his name – Anson. Ain't that the first name for Hawkstone? Yeah, I remember. Guess she was stuck on him.'

# EIGHTEEN

When Hawkstone and Black Feather rode in sunset back to the village, they found the old woman sitting cross-legged in front of her wickiup, rocking back and forth and wringing her hands. The wrinkled stone face held no expression, her lips were a straight, tight line. Her grief showed in her dark eyes. They looked up at Hawkstone with fear and loss and expectation.

'What is it?' he asked, standing down from the saddle.

She handed him the note. 'It tied to her pony.'

He held the note in both hands while he read that Hattie was taken as a hostage, and Hawkstone was to meet the marshal and Pearl Harp at her hotel room Wednesday morning eight o'clock. The wind wiggled the edges of the paper. As he took in the short, clipped words of Marshal Leather Yates, his jaw tightened and his breath quickened. He squinted, and his teeth clamped so tightly together they began to bring dull pain. He handed the note to Black Feather.

'My sister,' Black Feather said when he had read the note. His dark eyes gazed up and away to the west towards the burned shack. He wrinkled the note in his palm with both hands, kept crushing it until it became a tight, tiny ball. He threw the ball into the dead ashes of a cold camp fire. 'The trail is still fresh. She liked to go west in the afternoons. We start at the burned shack.'

'Let's git riding,' Hawkstone said.

\*

With open-oven biscuits and fresh canteen water, Hawkstone and Black Feather reached the timber skeleton when it was too dark to make out ground signs. They dismounted and walked around the shack.

Hawkstone said, 'We know where she was headed. She went to the Rio Gila for a swim and a bathe.'

Black Feather knelt on his left knee studying the ground. 'We do not know if she made the river.'

Hawkstone stood stiff, holding the reins of the chestnut in a tight fist. His teeth still ached from clenching. 'If they hurt her – if they did anything. . . .' He doubled his fist and held it in front of his face.

Black Feather stood and faced the fist. 'My brother, you have sailed the world and travelled the land. You know the way of men. You have watched these men, and you already know what they have done with our little Hattie.'

'Don't,' Hawkstone said. His voice broke and he had to clear his throat.

'You already know.'

Hawkstone sighed and nodded. 'Yes, we both know, especially these men. We can only hope she is still alive.'

'We can hope,' Black Feather said. He walked in a circle around the front of the charred timber skeleton his head bent to search the ground. 'We will sleep now. See better in daylight.'

In the morning, Black Feather studied hoofprints in the dewy earth. He walked slowly, leading his appaloosa stallion by the reins.

Hawkstone walked ahead with the chestnut. 'The pony was alone, no fresh tracks around.'

'No,' Black Feather said. 'They would wait for the river. They would want her without clothes.'

'Stop talking like that.'

'You can tell. You put off the believing, but you know.'

'Let's get to the river.'

Black Feather held up his palm. 'We will move slowly with the track of the appaloosa pony. They did not come close here, they held back. Here, between the shack and the river they kept their distance. I can backtrack the way from the village and pick up their horse prints. We rode over them last night.'

'I want to see the river,' Hawkstone said.

'You are anxious, my brother. Were you so anxious when you scouted for the cavalry?'

'It wasn't personal then,' Hawkstone said.

Sometime later, Black Feather swung down from his pony and bent with his knee to the ground. 'This was where they drifted behind to follow closer. You see the extra prints, the brown stain on the mesquite?'

'Tobacco juice,' Hawkstone said.

Black Feather nodded. 'From the spitter.' He remounted his horse and walked on.

'Wild Fletch Badger.' Hawkstone looked towards the river, still a mile away. 'They'd want to be close enough to watch her undress.'

'But she does not know. She rides on, no change in direction – the prints walking towards the water. She did not turn back to see what came after her.'

They rode silently over brown desert prairie grass thick with mesquite in places, by juniper with scraggly trunks, and around waist-high rocks until they saw willow and cottonwood ahead, and heard the light splash of running water from the Rio Gila river. The sun burned warm enough to have them reaching for their canteens when they reached the trees.

Hawkstone was the first to see the overlap of horse hoof-prints. 'This is where they caught up to her.'

Black Feather pointed to his right. 'There she take off clothes. She already in the water when they ride up. One sits on the bank to take off boots, here.' He walked a few steps. 'The dog, Volcano, ran here.' He walked on. 'He was shot here. He continues to run. Deep boot tracks of a fat man. See the blood. Volcano bit the fat man.'

'Marshal Leather Yates,' Hawkstone said.

'Volcano is dead. See entrails on mud.'

By studying tracks, Black Feather laid out the events that happened by the river. Hawkstone followed, and found tracks on his own across the river. He even held the tree branch she had used. Against his will he had to accept that Hattie Smooth Water was dragged back across the river and raped by three men. What he accepted more readily in his own mind was that the three men truly had only a short time to live. But that truth did not tell them where the men took Hattie when they had temporarily finished with her.

Knowing that their princess was no longer a maiden, that she had had her innocence brutally taken from her, churned at Hawkstone. He found himself breathing heavily through his nostrils, snorting like a Texas longhorn bull about to attack. His muscles felt tight, walking or riding. Though he fought the image, he pictured the three of them, their grimy hands on her, forcing her to allow them their pleasure. They would slap her, maybe even hit her. Forced to submit to the savage ways of such men, a victim of their brutality, and their numbers, she was completely helpless. They took what they wanted, then dragged her off – dragged her off to where?

Hawkstone and Black Feather sat on the bank, boots off, feet dipped in the river water. They smoked and passed the whiskey bottle back and forth.

Hawkstone said, 'Can you pick up the trail again?'

Black Feather stared at the flowing water. 'They clever,

ride back and forth, split, come together, go south across river, north back to burned shack, return towards village. It takes me days to find them.' He passed the bottle.

Hawkstone took a pull, then a drag from the cigarette. 'They sent Hattie's pony to the village with the note. That means they either already hid her away, or they had her with them and were packing double on one of the mounts.'

'I will know when I find tracks. If they pack double I see where they come from.'

'Can you pick them up from the village, from the pony?'

Black Feather rubbed his chin. 'Many tracks around the village, many ponies ride in and out. It will not be soon.'

Hawkstone turned to his blood brother. 'You're saying I got to ride with the hold-up. You telling me I got to ride with them rapists and not kill them right off.'

'We cannot destroy them until we find Hattie.'

'I know.'

'Or, at least know where she is.'

They sat silent, smoking and passing the bottle. When the vices were done with, both bottle and cigarette stubs were tossed in the current.

Hawkstone said, 'If I'm throwing in with the rapists, I got to find out if regulators are coming, and how many, and where they'll be. If that fella Roscoe told the bank about the hold-up, he mighta mentioned Steeple Rock, but he don't know the territory. The bank expects the stagecoach to be hit in New Mexico past Steeple Rock where the other hold-ups happened. Mebbe the regulators will wait there to surprise whatever bandits try.'

Black Feather leaned back on his elbows. 'When I find the trail and where it leads, I will ride for you. If you stay away from the hold-up, we must know the trail before next week.'

Hawkstone stood. 'I can't stay away now. They got me 'til

we find tracks. I don't know which trail Pearl Harp will take. I hope she rides on. But if she's there, I got to find some way to keep her away from the gunfire. You got to pick up the trail again, no matter how many days it takes.'

As they mounted, Black Feather said, 'These are bad *hombres*, my brother, they might try to gun you down at the stagecoach.'

'I'll be waiting.'

'So, you got a Franklin for them?'

'*When you talk to a man, watch his eyes. When he talks to you, watch his mouth.*'

# NINETEEN

Marshal Leather Yates thought to catch Pearl Harp still getting dressed, maybe in her unmentionables up there in her Wharton City hotel room, getting ready for him and Hawkstone. At seven-fifteen on Wednesday morning, activity in the hotel stirred slow and sour. The desk clerk with his vinegar face watched him come in and march for the stairs. Yates smelled coffee from the hotel restaurant kitchen, and wanted some. Inside his gut lay a pulsating fear that kept time with his heartbeat: what if Hawkstone knew about Hattie, the little princess? No, him and the Injun had been looking for almost a week and had found nothing. The previous night Yates had ridden out to pay a sugar call on Rocky Face Fiona and had checked the shack. Hattie's clothes were still there. The only question now was if Hawkstone would show at Pearl's room, ready for the hold-up.

When he knocked, Pearl opened the door fully dressed in buckskin with a cigarette stuck in the corner of her thin mouth, and her Colt Navy .36 strapped to her hip. She squinted against the smoke and opened the door wide. She wore a thin black overcoat – now open – to eventually hide her woman shape, her hair bundled under a plains hat. A blue kerchief was tied loose around her scrawny neck.

Yates hid his disappointment at not seeing her half-dressed or less, and went to a stand where she had a fresh pot of coffee, and helped himself. 'No Hawkstone?'

'He's downstairs ordering breakfast to be sent up.'

Yates raised his eyebrows. 'He was here last night?'

'All night long, you fat piece of hog.'

'Whoa, prison whore, just hold on. You don't talk to me like that.'

'He told me what you and your buzzards did to make him join in.'

'It was necessary.' The marshal squinted at her. 'Told you what?'

Pearl mashed out her cigarette and sat on the edge of the unmade bed. She picked up her coffee cup and sipped. 'How you got Hattie hid away someplace.'

'It will all work out, Pearl, so jest settle yourself.' The coffee tasted good. Pearl looked touchable in her skin-tight buckskin, but Yates figured he'd have nothing to do with Hawkstone's leavings – like sipping a greasy cup – her skinny neck red with whisker burns – no matter how tasty it looked. 'So, you're both in, and we ride out less than an hour from now. No time for a big breakfast.'

'Just toast and eggs. He wants me to ride away from this, go home.'

'But you ain't, right? We need you with us.'

Pearl put the cup down. 'Why? Four men is enough.'

The harder Yates looked at her, the less attractive she

became. It was that tough, experienced face and the neck done her in. She looked almost like a man. He found the track of his thinking went to just where and when they would shoot Pearl down. A ten- to fifteen-foot cliff overlooked the Rio Gila just before Steeple Rock. The land on the other side of the river was barren, without civilization. Her body might go over to follow the Apache princess and that torn mutt down into Mexico. Hawkstone would stay with the other bodies massacred by murdering thieving savages.

Marshal Leather Yates turned in the middle of the room with the coffee cup in his hand when the door flew open and Hawkstone stepped in. He looked at Pearl sitting on the bed and at the marshal. He took two steps and smashed his fist into the marshal's pork-chop whispered jaw.

Yates dropped the cup as he fell back against the footrail of the bed and rolled to the floor. He was clawing at his holster when he felt the business end of Hawkstone's Colt against his forehead.

'Where is she?' Hawkstone said.

From the bed, Pearl said, 'Don't kill him yet, Anson.'

'Why the hell not?'

'I need the money. We need the payroll.'

Hawkstone cocked the hammer on the Colt. 'I don't. I told you to go home. It ain't too late.'

Yates got his thinking straight after the shock. 'Kill me, and you'll never see the little princess again.'

'How about I just pistol whip you 'til you tell me where she is?'

'After this job we got to do, I'll take you to her.'

Yates waited. Hawkstone paused. He worked his jaws while his hazel eyes drilled a glare into the marshal. Tension eased when Hawkstone pulled the Colt and stood.

'Let's get it done, then,' Hawkstone said.

'After breakfast,' Pearl told him. 'I ain't robbin' no stage-coach on an empty stomach.'

From a bluff with the afternoon sun beating down on them, they watched the stagecoach roll away from the way station with fresh horses. Yates thought he heard gunshots, but he wasn't sure – they were too far away to know. That would be the boys taking care of the guards, likely back shooting them while they rested waiting for the stagecoach to roll out again.

'Let's go,' he said to Hawkstone and Pearl.

They mounted and rode hard towards Steeple Rock along the General's road. The marshal had scouted the rocks and found craggy breaks where they'd wait for the boys to catch up. Behind the rocks was enough space to leave the stagecoach when their business was done. They kept their horses with them tied to junipers. Across the road, mesquite grew on flat land to the cliff, with the flowing Rio Gila below.

The stagecoach, pulled by a brown four-up team, came in sight, swaying and rattling along the rough road, leaving a dusty, boiling wake. The driver watched for deep dips and tree trunks on the road. The shotgun slouched sleepy, with a rifle leaned against his leg pointed up.

Riding at full gallop, One Eye Tim Brace and Wild Fletch Badger closed distance behind the stagecoach.

'You hit the shotgun,' the marshal told Hawkstone. 'Me and Pearl will unload on the driver.'

'Better wait until the coach stops,' Hawkstone said, 'liable to have runaways.'

Before he finished the words, Yates saw One Eye fire and the shotgun rider pitched forward on to the back of a pulling brown and flopped under the coach. The left rear wheel rolled over his chest.

The driver pulled hard on the reins. 'Whoa there! Whoa!' The coach began to slow.

Wild Fletch fired the same time as Marshal Leather Yates. The driver spun left, then right, and pitched over to land on his head against a rock. Yates and Pearl and Hawkstone ran from the rocks. Hawkstone grabbed the reins of the lead brown to halt the coach. A stagecoach door opened. A fleshy-faced man in a light tan suit jumped out on to the road.

Hawkstone shouted, 'Fill your hand, Brennan!'

The copper mine vice president drew his Colt.

Yates noticed Hawkstone still hadn't drawn his weapon. Wild Fletch rode up on the left side of the coach, One Eye on the right. Gunfire came from inside. Wild Fletch grabbed his leg. The two riders opened fire on everyone inside. Brennen fired wild, chipping dirt, then aimed at Yates. Pearl shot Brennan through the head. Yates fired three times into the passenger compartment. After three shots each, the boys stopped firing. Pearl approached the stagecoach.

Yates saw Hawkstone pull and cock the hammer of his .45, aiming at the marshal, who twisted and shot Hawkstone's gun hand, and watched the Colt jerk away. Wild Fletch turned his mount from the stagecoach and shot Pearl twice in the face. Yates shot Hawkstone again, hitting a leg, and again somewhere in the torso. The lead horses jumped but did not take off running. One Eye aimed at Hawkstone's head and fired. The bullet went through the plains hat. Hawkstone tumbled down in the dirt by the hoofs of the lead horses, causing them to jerk back.

Yates looked inside the coach. A woman was bleeding from the chest. Three men bled over each other, two with drawn guns. One man in a blue suit and a handsome mustache moved. Yates shot him through the forehead. The marshal turned away from the coach and nodded to Pearl's body face down in the sandy dirt. 'Get her over the cliff. Got to move along, boys – no way of knowing who will come along.'

Still on their mounts, One Eye reloaded. Wild Fletch dismounted and tied his bandana around the bullet-creased leg. He remounted and pulled cartridges from his belt one at a time. The riders waited until they were finished reloading while the marshal glanced around the top of the coach looking for a payroll box.

Wild Fletch walked his horse along the coach. He bent from the saddle enough to pick up Pearl's leg. Still bent, he dragged the body to the cliff and dropped it over the side.

One Eye swung down from his saddle and pointed to Hawkstone lying in front of the stagecoach team. 'What about him?'

'Leave him where he is. Let's get that payroll. Look for a box or fat bags. You got the Apache stuff?'

'In tied bags,' Wild Fletch said, riding back from the cliff. He dismounted at the stage and pulled two hefty bags from the back of his mount.

'Start sticking arrows where they fit, and swing tomahawks.' Yates pointed to the body of Brennan in the brown suit. 'Scalp that vice-president. We can't dawdle, boys. Them regulators mighta heard some of the shooting. We don't know how far away they are, and they could come riding fast.'

Marshal Leather Yates began his search as the boys stuck arrows into bodies, and jammed them into the side of the coach. Sweating in southwest sunshine, they worked quickly, sniffing and coughing, getting blood on their hands and clothes. Wild Fletch did not hesitate to slice off the boot heel piece of hair and flesh from the top of Brennan's head. Since One Eye had no stomach for it, Wild

Fletch buried the tomahawk deep into the woman's face. She wore a gold band, which he took. As an afterthought, he ripped open the front of her dress, and smiled his approval at what he saw.

They wrenched open carpet bags and suitcases, dragged the bodies out and yanked seats apart. When they had stripped all the luggage from on top of the coach, Marshal Yates stood back breathing hard, with his bloody hands on his hips.

'We been outfoxed, boys.' He looked from one to the other. 'More like we been betrayed.'

One Eye said, 'That bottle-eye mouse.'

Wild Fletch took a bite of tobacco and slapped his good leg. 'Roscoe Dees. He went and blabbed about the plan.'

Yates nodded. 'Got hisself to the bank, not Santa Fe, and poured out his soul for five hundred back-stab cash. Let's see what these gents are carrying.'

After they stripped wallets and purse the total came to eight hundred and forty-two dollars.

'Don't hardly seem worth it,' Yates said. He looked back along the road. 'We better push these folks back in and get this coach outta sight. We'll take the team 'cause that's what the Injuns would have done.'

One Eye gawked along the string of the four-team with his one good eye. 'Hey!'

Yates stared at him. 'The regulators coming?'

'Look!'

As they watched, the chestnut mare galloped by at full speed, Hawkstone leaned over with both hands gripping the saddle horn, riding hard for the edge of the cliff.

The three men pulled their weapons and opened fire, splitting the hot air with a staccato of gunfire until they clicked empty.

'I hit him,' One Eye said.

Marshal Leather Yates watched as the chestnut disappeared over the cliff. 'I think we all hit him. No need for concern, boys. Anson Hawkstone is done for.'

# TWENTY

When Hawkstone hit the river it was as if a solid door slapped him. He went down quickly as the slow current caught him, the water making his bleeding wounds sting with pain. He couldn't count how many times he had been shot. His head felt as if it had been carved with a tomahawk, making him flow in and out of consciousness. His hat was gone. The chestnut mare swam ahead, kicking hoofs, looking for anywhere she could walk out on firm ground.

The water close around Hawkstone turned scarlet against the otherwise grey river. He pushed his head up to breathe, only to dip down again and drift with the current. Being lighter, he started to catch up the chestnut. Stone walls dominated to the left; to the right a desert of sagebrush and mesquite sloped down to meet the river. An envelope of pressure closed around him.

Something brushed his face. He jerked in fear, thinking it was Pearl's hair. Dizziness made him slip his head under water. But she was far downstream, too far to catch unless her body caught on something. He forced his head into air and blew water from his nostrils, and coughed. He breathed shallow as he flowed.

His face felt the brush again. It was the chestnut's tail. Hawkstone had no feeling in his shot right hand, along with other numb areas. He grabbed a fistful of tail with his left, and held tight, strung behind as a fish caught behind a canoe, his head flashing dark and light, unable to see. The chestnut continued to kick her legs under him while she aimed for shore. Her front hoofs touched the bank on the right. She slipped in sandy mud, but lunged ahead, pulling with her front legs, pushing with her back hoofs, digging in, moving up, dragging her rider behind her on to the slick wet shore, then dry mesquite and desert covered with sage grass.

He wasn't aware when his left hand let go of the chestnut's tail. He came back to himself in short bursts, and whenever he did so, he felt the chestnut still close. He felt the hot sun turn his blood-soaked clothes sticky to his skin. Another time he shivered in a night chill. His throat felt parched, but he lacked the strength to turn around and crawl to the river for drink. His stomach gurgled with hunger. He wanted a cigarette, and a swallow of whiskey. Mostly he wanted his leaks patched. Mentally, during an awake time, he counted six wounds, mostly creases because he was moving while they shot. The left shoulder was the worst because the bullet didn't go through. The head crease hurt most and made him dizzy. The right hand and arm had no feeling. A chunk of meat was torn from his side, and another crease had hit his right leg just above the knee. They all bled, and he had no way to stop them.

In between his ability to think and reason, his mind turned black without thoughts. He woke surprised by sunshine, or darkness. He tried to move, but he had lost too much blood. Life continued to dribble out of him. When next he woke he tried to think logically. There had been no days and nights. There had been half a day, and one night.

As a dark night chill crept through his bones he forced

himself to move. The head wound seemed to bleed the most. The greatest pain came from his shoulder. He turned to push his head against sand, trying to slow the bleeding. He could have used his bandana to wrap his head tight, but no other part of him would move, not arms or legs, and certainly not his right hand. He lay on his belly, his head turned to the side, consciously pushing it against sand. He still felt nothing of his right hand or arm.

At times, he drifted in a half-dream world. Pictures of his past streamed behind his eyes. He thought of Hattie, of course – did she huddle with fear in some dark place, wondering and hoping somebody might find her – did she pray for Black Feather or Hawkstone to break in and sweep her back home? And Pearl, her girl body jerked by bullets slamming into it, then lying dead by the stagecoach – now drifted away and gone forever. That hurt because he had warned her, told her to go home. She hadn't listened and was dead now, long gone, leaving him with a feeling of loss.

For reasons he could not explain, the face of Rachel Good Squaw emerged and stayed with him. He remembered holding her in that cave years ago when he was married to somebody else – to Susan, with his son, Michael. He had wanted Rachel then, and had thought about coming to her. But when he found his family blown to pieces by bank robbers, he knew it was too late for any kind of good life, with Rachel or anyone else, because he turned outlaw and became no good, as a man, even as a human being. Eventually he had gone to prison, and that had ended any chance with her.

'Rachel,' he croaked, 'Rachel,' saying her name, but knowing the sound was wasted.

Gone again to black non-thinking, what seemed like days passed in an hour or two and he dreamed again, dreamed of his world-girdling shipmate, Ben Coral. Ben had known

Rachel when she was Rachel Cleary, a slim, red-headed girl of sixteen and in love with Ben's shipmate, Anson Hawkstone. The lads went to sea and the girl stayed behind, in the family way, but this unknown to them – an orphan, her baby girl stillborn, off to business school, then capture by savages. The world of the Apache became her life.

Why did he think of those soft warm days and nights now? Was it because he had come to face death? Did he want to remember the loving, softest parts of his life?

If he wasn't going to die, he'd better start thinking where those animals kept Hattie. And he'd better lay out in what slow and agonizingly painful way the three of them would meet their end.

He came out of his dream world to a dark, harsh, painful reality. Off to his right among willows, the chestnut shook her head, rattling her reins. Her moon shadow stepped to the river and noisily slurped a drink. She came to nuzzle his spine, and moved her wet nose to the back of his neck. She stood close. She snorted the last drops of water from her nostrils. Then out of the corner of his eye he saw her head go up and her ears point forwards. He could not lift his head enough to see more, but in the ground he felt the pound of hoofs as a horse approached at a gallop.

Anson Hawkstone went out again and felt, rather than saw, what happened to him. He caught a glimpse of an old man, an Apache, not quite as wrinkled as the old woman, but almost. He rode in shadow. A blank period took over and passed through Hawkstone's head. His body was moved, lifted with grunts and the smell of man sweat and outhouse and wood smoke. Night passed with the Apache building something using willow and cottonwood limbs tied with leather straps – a travois. The travois stretched in a triangle, the narrow end tied to the chestnut's saddle horn, the wide end on the ground. Between were stretched more limbs covered with leaves and grass. Hawkstone had been lifted on to it. The right sleeve of his shirt hung torn from wrist to armpit. His buckskin pants carried a slit to show the shot leg. Cloth had been wrapped around his waist and another strip about his head. All the wounds smelled of cavalry latrine leavings and dead animal and river mud, and he knew not what else. A paste of it covered each tear in his body. He was given a cup of water that he gulped quickly.

'More,' he croaked.

'Enough,' the old man said. 'I say how much.'

In morning sunshine, Hawkstone felt he was leaving again, going away to the darkness. 'Black Feather,' he whispered.

'Yes,' the old man said. He went away from sight and mounted his swayback pinto and began to move, pulling the reins of the chestnut, the travois dragging behind. The chestnut still carried the Mexican saddle, the saddle not completely dry yet from the river.

The sun began to heat the land, while Hawkstone felt himself dragged and bumped over dips and hollows and through small canyons. He went in and out of his conscious self.

'Rachel,' he said.

'Yes,' he heard the old man answer from ahead. 'What Rachel?'

Hawkstone did not know what the old Apache meant. He bounced and grimaced in pain, and hissed through his teeth as sharp pins of agony pierced him. But the smelly paste seemed to be working, because as the day wore on, the bleeding had stopped and the pain appeared to lessen. His thinking almost came back to normal. But he still could not move.

They stopped, and the old Apache gave him another cup

111

of water and some deer jerky to munch. Hawkstone saw the old man clearly now. Dressed in loose, filthy Apache buckskin, his forehead looked as if it had once been scalped. A wide patch of scar pushed beyond a beaded headband. His eyes were deep and black into a thin wrinkled face with a large hook nose and full mouth. A worm-thick knife scar went across his throat just under his jaw. The dark eyes were flanked by deep wrinkles that went deeper as he squinted against sun glare. He had no front teeth.

'I am Moving Rock,' he said.

'Where do you take me?'

'To the medicine woman – in your babble you want medicine woman.'

'What medicine woman?'

'In the village, half day ride from Fort McLane. Rachel. You croak for her. Rachel Good Squaw, the white woman with the sunset hair, the medicine woman.'

# TWENTY-ONE

Anson Hawkstone slept lightly, vaguely aware of village noise – children mostly, and dogs, and the prance of ponies and the voices of women who talked with their men, a soft murmur when they spoke with each other, a coo while they cradled their babies.

A woman close said, 'Help me get him inside.'

'Rachel,' Hawkstone said, his voice raw with emotion. He barely believed it was her.

'Hush yourself,' she told him.

112

He blinked, tried to focus, but the night and his head kept him fuzzy. Two men lifted him off the travois and carried him into a sod hut, and laid him on blankets spread to the floor. He felt the warmth of burning mesquite and juniper from a fireplace. A lantern hung close to a wall and spread a golden glow to the one-room hut. The men left. A girl he took to be Hattie bent over him and picked at the paste covering his wounds. She was too young to be Hattie. He touched her arm with his good left hand. He wanted to say something but no words came.

She smiled at him, looking angelic in the glow. 'I am Little Rain. We wash you. We take care of you now. We make you better.'

'Moving Rock,' Hawkstone said.

'The old man is gone. He does not care for people.'

The girl and Rachel cut away his clothes. After the girl had cleaned the wounds, Rachel examined each gash.

'We can't burn the side or head. I got catgut – looks like six stitches for your side and four to close the head crease. Fetch the knife from the fire, Little Rain.'

Hawkstone knew what was coming. 'Get me a stick.'

The girl brought a cut willow limb the diameter of a dog leg, about eight inches long. Hawkstone put it between his teeth. Without hesitation, Rachel pressed the hot knife against the leg and arm wounds and kept it there, sliding it, making him growl as he bit hard on the limb. His eyes flooded with tears, blocking his vision as he roared against the stick. The smell was of frying meat, but not sweet like cooking game – a rusty, sour smell, the smell of a house of burning people, or the smell of an Apache village after the cavalry have finished killing and are burning everything.

Rachel said, 'Your hand will heal on its own.' She paused and stared at him, looking misty through his tears. 'You done bawling?'

With his left hand he pulled the stick. 'Git it done.'

'Little Rain, put the knife back in the fire,' Rachel said. She turned back to Hawkstone. 'We got to get that bullet outta your shoulder. It's stuck in a bone.'

Little Rain returned and held the lantern close to his shoulder. The limb went back in his mouth. Rachel began to probe with a thin knife. Hawkstone shut his eyes tight against the pain, letting tears flow. His teeth clamped stiff against the limb. He growled with a bellow that filled the hut, and roared again. She had to be using a hatchet – digging for the bullet with a shovel. He snarled and jerked while the spindly girl, Little Rain, tried to hold him. She couldn't, and Rachel pressed her knee down on his arm to hold it still.

'Got it,' she said. 'Quickly, Little Rain, bring me the hot knife.'

Hawkstone's thinking went black.

In the morning he woke clear-headed. The fire of pain in his body burned deepest from the left shoulder. Rachel Cleary, now Rachel Good Squaw, dressed in a buckskin skirt to her knees and calf moccasins, and a beaded linen shirt, sat beside him on the dirt floor, cross-legged in the Apache way. She pulled the blanket higher along his chest to his throat. She smiled. Her red hair grew wild out and around her head and down to her shoulder blades, but now there were streaks of grey in the flow of it. Her face showed a per-manent flush, oval and smooth except for tiny wrinkles along the sides of her blue eyes, eyes as blue as a china cup. The single-line tattoo ran from her lower lip to the bottom of her chin. Her hand rested on his shoulder, elegant with long fingers.

Hawkstone felt his right arm again. He raised it. 'The hand.'

'You'll get feeling back in a day or two. The bullet went between the knuckles. The wrap is tight.'

He pushed his left arm out of the blanket and touched her knee. 'It is good to see you again, woman. I heard you moved, but not where. You look good.'

More tiny wrinkles worked the edges of her mouth when she smiled. 'I'm forty now, Anson. I help heal from what I picked up over the years, but I reckon I'm less desirable these days.'

'*Great modesty often hides great merit,*' Hawkstone said.

She sat back and he saw fondness in her blue eyes. 'Do you still do that?'

'Benjamin Franklin? Yup. What I can remember. I ain't always exact.'

She leaned over and kissed his cheek. 'You'll be with us a spell, Anson Hawkstone. You lost too much blood. You rest a few days.'

'You may be the medicine woman, but I got to ride out soon. Men got to be dealt with.'

'I'll say when you ride,' Rachel said. She pointed a finger at him. 'You listen to me.'


He went in and out of sleep as the pain in his wounds diminished. Rachel had a string of Apache visitors, children with sniffles and stomach aches, pregnant women and girls, young men with bullet wounds. The girl Little Rain tended to Hawkstone. She changed bandages that covered scabs from the hot knife, and the wrap around his waist and head, and when he woke she waited with a cup of water. She brought him cooked goat, and rabbit, and venison. She was young and graceful and easy to look at, and she smelled of deep mountain forest and pine needles. She reminded him so much of Hattie, and his need to get moving clawed at him.

115

During the second evening Hawkstone, now able to sit, and Rachel sat in the lantern glow and spoke softly of the last time they were together, and what had happened to them in the years between. He told her of his life with the Apache, and of prison and the stage hold-up, and who had shot him up. She told him of the move, and how several older braves had wanted her, and had offered her animals and gold to take them as her man. But what they wanted was her long-legged, full-bodied shape, and to be waited on by her, and she discovered she did not need a man to live a comfortable, satisfying life.

She kept busy, and she stayed with the Apache because she could not live with the Christian judgments in the white man's world. Most supplies not available in the village she could get from Fort McLane. As they spoke she allowed him to keep his hand against the inside of her bare leg above the moccasin, and twice, before she crossed to her own bed, she left him with a warm wet kiss that got him stirred.

In the morning of his third day, Hawkstone heard and saw Rachel talking with a rugged Apache warrior who stood outside her door.

The warrior paced back and forth in front of her. 'I, Great Eagle, have been patient with you, Rachel Good Squaw. You know I have not pressed you for an answer.'

'You've been patient,' she said. 'Even when I told you I got no interest.'

'You do have interest. I see it in your eyes.'

'You see what you wish, not what is there.'

Great Eagle pointed behind her to the inside of the hut. 'Who is he, this Anson Hawkstone? Will he be your man?'

'Yes, when he has put himself back together.'

'I have offered you horses and pigs and a better hut, and the company of my two boys. What can he offer you?'

'History. He brings me a time of happy years when a

young girl was in love. We have many years when we should have been together.'

'He will stay with you?'

'No, he will leave me. But he will come back and he will stay with me for a spell. He will always come back.'

Great Eagle stopped, lips tight, black, deep-set eyes glaring. 'You cannot live with a sometime man, gone to the wind and coming back for your favours, then gone again.'

'Yes I can. I want it that way.'

'You need all-time man, a man to lie with every night, a man to look after, to cook for, to tend his children, to provide his needs.'

'As heavenly as that sounds for a woman, I do not need any of it. I find that most of the time men are a demanding nuisance. I am the medicine woman. That is enough for me. When the Hawkstone man is with me, I will enjoy him. When he goes away I will think good riddance, but I will wish him well and look forward to his return so I can enjoy him until he leaves again.'

'Ah, you a stupid woman.'

Rachel sighed. 'Why would Great Eagle want a stupid woman?'

Great Eagle shook his head and stomped away.

Rachel came back inside the hut. Little Rain washed her patient's face with a wet cloth. She turned, her black hair down to her waist like Hattie's, and faced Rachel.

When Rachel saw Hawkstone sitting on the blankets watching her, she put her hands on her hips. 'I'll have no blustery wind from you, Anson Hawkstone.'

'I am speechless,' Hawkstone told her. 'What man can know the thoughts that carry a woman?'

Little Rain said, 'This one will be your man, Rachel?'

'I intend to keep him.' She stepped to Hawkstone while Little Rain scurried out of the way. She looked down at him.

Her red hair looked on fire from morning sunshine coming through the door. 'I suppose you think you get special favours now I spilled myself out.'

Hawkstone placed his left hand on the calf of her moccasin. 'I suppose I do.'

'Tonight you will move yourself to share my bed. I will be gentle with you – at first.' Though her face looked stern, the corners of her mouth worked up a little to a smile.

'Rider coming in the village,' Little Rain said, looking out of the open doorway.

Hawkstone could not see outside with willowy Little Rain and shapely Rachel blocking the way. A grip squeezed his chest. He caught glimpses of an appaloosa's legs as they passed. The painful shoulder announced itself from his movement to see. The horse went into the village.

Rachel turned to him and saw his expression. 'You know that Apache, Anson?'

'I think so. He comes here.'

Rachel went back to the doorway as the appaloosa approached. 'Do you look for Hawkstone?'

'Yes, he is my blood brother,' the rider said. 'Is he inside?'

Rachel stood back and Black Feather entered carrying full saddle-bags, and looked down at Hawkstone. 'You are alive.'

'You took your sweet time tracking me.'

'The river slowed me. I brought your money, ten thousand, from the first robbery, the Mineral City bank.' Black Feather dropped the saddle-bags next to Hawkstone. He carried the scent of his horse and the outside air and the trail, and a dark brooding cloud on his face. He knelt and put his hand on Hawkstone's arm. 'I got to get back to the village. The smell of events is bad. But I must tell you, my brother, our little sister, Hattie Smooth Water, is dead.'

# TWENTY-TWO

Wharton City Marshal Leather Yates did not try to hide his frustration. Getting a decision from the army at Fort Grant was like riding a horse backwards. Anything to do with government was the same. But they had to move on the village before word reached it and they found help. He told nobody that he and his two deputies had left the stagecoach behind the rocks with the passengers inside to smell up the landscape. There was enough evidence – Lieutenant Horatio Crock clearly saw the work of Apache when the marshal showed him the scene. Lieutenant Crock did not impress Leather Yates at all. He reminded the marshal of a desk clerk in a bank, with his immaculate uniform and baby face and spare boyish frame – maybe early twenties, with about as much life experience as a schoolgirl.

Yates explained, as they studied the stagecoach aftermath, the village where the renegades came from was not far, out along Disappointment Creek. The cavalry, the four regulators from the bank, the marshal and his two deputies had to move fast.

Now, it had been a week since the hold-up, and the lieutenant still waited for orders from his colonel, who was somewhere north with a campaign against hostiles around the copper mines. Yates sat in the waiting room six days straight. He sweated and grew hungry and thirsty with not enough food and drink while he waited for a decision. His deputies kept an eye on the village, one ready to ride hard

119

to him if any alarm went out.

Yates' biggest concern now was the news from Rocky Face Fiona that Black Feather, sidekick to the late deceased Hawkstone, had tracked their trail to the Way Out Saloon and found the clothes of the demised princess in the shack. But worse was what his deputies who were watching the tribe saw: a brave from downriver who rode into the village with the girl's body over a spare pinto. She hadn't flowed far down the river, maybe got snagged on some outgrowth, so the braves in the village knew the princess had been raped and killed, and they'd have a real grouch on – especially that Black Feather fella who might get warriors together.

On the seventh day the marshal at last learned that the lieutenant had received instructions from his colonel via a worn-out rider: attack the village. Try to spare women and children. Burn everything. Dispense with those responsible for the stagecoach massacre.

Yates learned that before word about the stagecoach massacre – as it became called – circulated through army barracks, the one woman aboard had been brutally raped by at least twenty savages and murdered with a tomahawk to the face. By the third day after the news, the number had grown from twenty to forty, and the woman went from hardware store wife to young nun.

Once a decision had been made as to when they would attack, Marshal Yates relaxed. He met his two deputies, One Eye Tim Brace and Wild Fletch Badger at the Way Out Saloon. The first thing they noticed at the shack was that the clothes of the princess were still there, undisturbed.

Wild Fletch spat to the floor. His buzzard face glanced around at three men drinking before he looked hard at the marshal. 'We got no payday. Eight hundred dollars ain't gonna cut, Marshal. ' 'Specially after we been talking to them regulators.'

Yates squinted at him. 'What about the regulators?'

One Eye lifted his hat brim enough to give the marshal a cyclops stare. 'We talked to this fella, this Two Handle Rowdy Smith. He carries a pair of pearl-handled Peacemakers, like that federal marshal.' One Eye sat back in his chair. 'You know why some of them gunfighters carries two guns?'

'Showing off,' Yates said.

One Eye grinned with self-satisfaction. 'Nope. It's on account of the Colt Peacemaker sometimes don't hit on a cylinder, it misfires, don't shoot when it's supposed to. Then another gun can be pulled and blasted away.'

The marshal stared at One Eye. 'Why do you think that is?'

Wild Fletch spat. 'Dunno, bad design.'

The marshal rolled and lit a smoke. 'It's 'cause men like you – and likely this Rowdy fella – ain't clean. Look at you. Dirty clothes, dirty skin, dirty hair – even a dirty mind. And a dirty weapon. You don't clean yourselves, and you don't keep your pistol clean. That's why it will misfire.'

Wild Fletch pushed the wad of tobacco to his left cheek. 'We're ridin' all over the countryside doin' one thing and another, we ain't got time for a clean. All we can do is wet our whistle once in a while, and get a poke if we're lucky.'

One Eye looked out of the pulled curtain door. 'You know what else Two Handle Rowdy told us? He says to me and Fletch here that somebody done took that payroll money.'

Marshal Yates twisted his head so fast he almost lost his hat. 'What?'

Both deputies nodded. 'The bank ain't sayin' nothing about it. It was a week before the stagecoach, not the day before. They sent it in a wagon, and the wagon got held up.'

Yates frowned. 'The spectacle clerk would have known.'

'Mebbe,' Fletch said. He spat. 'Only the clerk got no reason to tell us. He don't like us so much since we didn't pay him his five hundred dollars. But that ain't the all of it.'

'What do you mean?' the marshal said.

'Whoever robbed the wagon come up empty like we done the stagecoach.' One Eye said. 'The money was really in saddle-bags riding fast overland with fresh horses, like the old Pony Express. *That's* what was held up.'

'By who?' the marshal asked.

Wild Fletch spat what was left of his wad towards the doorway. 'A woman drivin' the wagon and the two guards and the fellas holding a fresh horse all said the same thing: four riders, three of them Injun.'

Marshal Leather Yates slapped the table. 'Anson Hawkstone!'

'That's how we figure,' One Eye said. 'He come with us on the hold-up on account of the princess, but he already had the payroll money, only we don't know where.'

The marshal rubbed his whiskered jowls. 'The burned-out house.'

The deputies shook their heads. 'No,' One Eye said. 'We figure he hid it with his tribe, that village he belongs to, in one of them tepees.'

The marshal looked from one to the other. 'You boys know what we got to do when we hit that village.'

Wild Fletch said, 'It's gonna be hard. He coulda buried it anywhere around them tepees. And we can't ask the man on account of he's already dead.'

'His sidekick, Black Feather, ain't dead,' the marshal said.

Four days later, they bunched outside the north-east area of the village just after dawn. The lieutenant had told Yates that ten horse soldiers should be able to do the job. There would be the four regulators and the two deputies and Yates to back them.

The village stirred with morning fires started. Animals made impatient noises for attention and food. The smell of them mixed with burning wood in still, dew-dripping air. Smoke rose slightly from greenwood fires and hung there with no wind to carry it off. Yates sat his horse next to the lieutenant and caught a glimpse of warriors darting between tepees, carrying rifles. He felt a slam of fear hit his chest.

'Lieutenant,' he said – and no more.

'Attack!' the lieutenant shouted. With the order barely out of his mouth, he was immediately shot and fell dead to the ground.

'Kill them all!' Yates bellowed. As riders leaped their mounts forwards to descend on the village, weapons began firing, men shouted, the crack and snap of gunfire rolled across tepees and echoed off nearby hills. Yates pulled the reins to hold his horse back, but it didn't want to stay back – it kept lunging forwards with the others. Yates yanked hard until the last rider galloped into the village, firing left and right. His mount settled.

One Eye Tim Brace and Wild Fletch Badger rode at the front, shooting children first, then young mothers, then women – any human that moved in front of them. They rode into tepees to empty their pistols, then leaped with their mounts just outside the carnage to reload and return. Old men and women, young men and boys were gunned down. Most ran from the bluecoats to drop in their steps. Brave warriors fired their rifles until they ran out of cartridges, then used the weapons as clubs. Five of the ten horse soldiers fell dead, one regulator was killed. Shouts of hate dominated louder than the screams of women as they ran. Children yelped when shot, then died in silence.

Yates watched from the safety of the village edge.

The coldest killers, besides his deputies, were the regulators, whom he reckoned were no more than outlaw quick-draw, kill-for-hire gunmen. The invaders loaded and emptied their rifles and pistols. Apache fell and were trampled by running horses. Even animals were not spared – dogs, pigs, goats, chickens jerked as hot lead sliced into them. A couple of young, inexperienced men of the army quickly lost the excitement of slaughter, and with tears sliding down their cheeks, rode outside the village to stare.

Marshal Yates figured them to be cowards.

Neither soldiers nor regulators spared older girls and young women aged fourteen to twenty. With the village burning and littered with bodies, four girls were yanked up to a rider's saddle and ridden off along Disappointment Creek. One of the riders along the creek included the sergeant now in charge with the lieutenant dead. No orders were issued to stop. The snap and clip of gunfire ceased when there was nothing more to kill, or burn. Tepees quickly blazed with the dead animal smell of buffalo hide to blend with the rusty odour of butchery. Smoke rose wide and high, and hung because no breeze had started yet. Two sweating soldiers rode slowly through the bodies to fire bullets into those still with a flicker of life.

The entire episode took eight minutes.

Marshal Yates sat back in the saddle, his hands shaking on the saddle horn as he tingled with excitement. He found himself rocking back and forth in the saddle, hissing in and out through his teeth. A private rode up to him, sweating, with splatters of blood over his uniform and face.

Yates pulled off his bowler and ran his hand over his scalp. 'That'll teach 'em to massacre a stagecoach.'

The private's young face wrinkled in disgust. 'Where the hell was you, fat man?' He rode on to another spot and held up his arm for others to see. With the sergeant having ridden off to the creek with a girl, there were just three other cavalrymen who joined the private.

Yates did not like the sting of the words. The cavalry patrol had lost half their men – but, he reckoned, they should have sent more, at least twenty. Still, they made a good account of themselves, killing off thirty-eight hostiles – maybe four warriors. All three of the surviving regulators and his two deputies had gone off to have sport – and why not? They deserved the spoils of victory.

Marshal Yates rode easy into the village. Smoke blocked vision like a black shroud. The payroll was buried someplace, either under one of the tepees or nearby. He dismounted and poked his boot around. He found a silver buckle with a silver dotted belt, and picked it up. He looped it over his shoulder. There were gold bracelets and silver necklaces he put in his pockets. The boys would return soon after their girly business. He knew from personal experience that kind of action didn't take long. They'd be back and maybe ready to dig for the payroll. Or, they could return another time. The killing was sure enough done for now.

And after the killing, came the looting.

One nagging thought buzzed through the marshal's head as he rubbed the stinging dog bite on the back of his leg and mounted his horse. He had reckoned that the end of the village would sever all connection with Anson Hawkstone and any threat to his life – but he hadn't seen the body of the old woman or Black Feather anywhere. No sign of them.

# TWENTY-THREE

Anson Hawkstone stood inside the shack behind Way Out Saloon. He held Hattie Smooth Water's clothes while his chest and guts felt shredded as if a grizzly had clawed and chewed his entrails. He had trouble swallowing.

Black Feather stood by the wood-planked weather-worn door – the only light came from gaps between the boards. 'I keep them here so you can see. They did not bring her here. They killed her on the bank and pushed her in the river. Children at a tribal village near Mineral Creek found Hattie – one or two knew she was from our tribe. A warrior brought her to us. We sent her to spirits in other clothes. These carry their scent. They held these and sniffed them before they raped her. We will burn them.'

'The old woman?' Hawkstone asked.

'She is in the hills that reach for the Pinon Llano mountains with Burning Buffalo. She weeps with grief. We must get to the village. Bad medicine, my brother, I do not like what might happen. Spirits make me fear what has already happened.'

They rode as fast as Hawkstone's wounds would allow – a trot, an easy gallop, finally walking their mounts. He had new clothes from Fort McLane to cover his bandages – Levi jeans with copper rivets at the pocket corners, a yellow light wool shirt and a black leather vest, a new Colt .45 Peacemaker, and a grey plains hat to cover the wrap around his head. His saddle scabbard held a Winchester '76. His boots were still good, and he rode the chestnut mare with the Mexican saddle. They crossed the Rio Gila and rode slowly up Disappointment Creek.

The smell came at them first.

Hawkstone had not recovered from the rape and murder of Hattie. He carried her clothes in his saddle bags to be burned. When he caught the deadly odour of the village a burn stuck in his throat and his chest fluttered which made him foresee a dreaded sight – but the scene before his eyes did not prepare him for the carnage. The tepees at the edge were not there. No crows cawed from tree branches. No dogs barked. The first of the bodies lay in front of them. As they rode in, bodies spread among cold ashes the length of the village like mesquite bushes across the flat desert. A chill ran through him. Any substance in his chest sunk to the pit of his stomach. The chestnut walked uneasily, stepping carefully.

Black Feather walked his appaloosa silently beside Hawkstone. He pointed to a body with no forehead. 'Jimmy Wolfinger.' He nodded to a pile of ash. 'My tepee was there.'

They looked left and right as their horses walked. Hawkstone recognized bodies, even some of the dogs. He tried to breathe shallow because of the smell. He looked up to see Federal Marshal Casey Steel sitting his mount in front of a ruin that had once been the old woman's wickiup.

As they approached, Steel said, 'What stirred up the cavalry to do something like this?'

'Not here,' Hawkstone said. 'I ain't talking here.' He reined the chestnut to the right, away from the village to the big boulders along Disappointment Creek, beyond the bodies of four girls taken there. Steel and Black Feather followed.

They sat on boulders and pulled Bull Durham and corn paper and rolled smokes. Hawkstone leaned back against a rock. Every part of his body ached with patched bullet-hole stings. His heart and head felt numb.

Marshal Casey Steel studied Hawkstone. 'What happened to you?'

Hawkstone said nothing.

The marshal looked from one to the other. 'I got two wagons of prisoners coming from Yuma Territorial for burial detail. It will have to be a mass grave. You got anyone special, you got to say.'

Black Feather and Hawkstone inhaled cigarette smoke and remained silent.

Steel slid off his black Montana Peak Stetson and rubbed his thinning hair. He returned his hat. 'I talked to the sergeant who took over the raid after his lieutenant got shot down. He says five of the ten soldiers got cut down. The cavalry had help. He talked about four bank regulators – one killed – and a town marshal and his two deputies. The marshal had come upon a stagecoach that was attacked by Apache.'

Despite his pain, Hawkstone felt grateful to the marshal. He was naming victims for them, saying how many cavalry soldiers and regulators there were, and those who plundered the village – the killing looters who would have to die.

Steel tightened his lips and looked back and forth. 'Anything you fellas can tell me? Anything at all?' He waited. He flipped his cigarette into the creek. 'I'm gonna have a talk with the bankers in Tucson. Something ain't right about all this. If them Apache was from this village and they held up the stagecoach and killed them people, then they came back here with the money the stagecoach was carrying. How much was it? Where is it? That was a private stage run by Longfellow Copper. So, my guess is they was running payroll out to the mines. Some braves in this here village held it up and come back with the money. The city marshal found the stagecoach and them stinking bodies and went running to the cavalry, mebbe figuring to get the money back. I don't know if them regulators work for the bank or Longfellow. Either way the regulator gunmen had to have a reason to jump on the raid. I reckon they was paid. What do you think it was? Who do you think paid them regulator fellas?'

Black Feather flipped his spent smoke into the creek. He looked at the marshal then beyond him towards the village. He pulled his Colt and rotated the cylinders, checking the load. His black hair fell to each side of his face, hiding it. He said nothing.

Steel turned to Hawkstone. 'You fellas can start talking my ears off anytime now. You ain't doing yourself no good keeping shut. What do you know about what's going on?'

Hawkstone smoked the last of his cigarette. He mashed his boot heel on it against the boulder and glared at the marshal. He grimaced and twitched with a shot of pain, and twisted his back. A wind had come up blowing across the tribal village away from the creek. The wind diminished the smell but did not eliminate it. Three buzzards flew past above them, their wings angled towards the carnage. He said nothing to the marshal.

Federal Marshal Casey Steel stood on his boulder, pulled off his Stetson again and slapped his leg with it. 'Want you to know it was real pleasant chatting with you fellas.' He pointed his finger from one to the other. 'What you keep from me is goin' to come back like a rattler. It's gonna bite you with a poison that will either put you in a prison cell or kill you. Mark me, the pair of you.'

They watched the marshal step shakily down from the boulders in his high boot heels, walk his bowed stubby legs back to the village, mount up and ride out.

Hawkstone laid his head back on the boulder. He heard the wind rustle cottonwood branches and the splash of the fast-moving creek. He thought of Rachel Good Squaw and her touch and her response to his touch. He had left the money Black Feather brought with her. He trusted her without knowing why. She affected any decision he made now. The decisions he was about to make would bring changes he could not reverse, changes that would alter the course of his life for all the days he had left.

'I wasn't going back to this,' he told Black Feather.

Black Feather squinted, looking at whitewater. 'Does my brother think we have choices?'

'I reckon not. It's jest, before prison I was one kind of man. I don't know what kind. I don't know what I was. Not a man, not human. Jest some sort of predator animal taking up space and doing harm to others. Not much good for nothing. I deserved prison. Only chance and luck kept me from getting hung. I would have deserved that too, the things I done. Ain't no forgiveness for what I was and how I acted. When I got out I was a different kind of man. No more outlaw trail. No more killing for the sake of killing. I was gonna take the money they sent me to prison for and make a different life. Mebbe ride a hard, lonely trail but make it a good one, a decent one.'

'You think that is beyond you now? Away in a land you cannot find?'

'Mebbe, mebbe not. When we do what we gotta do, I may go back to what I once was, be no good again. I found Rachel and that might redeem me. Could be I was meant to ride the lonesome trail, ride alone. But I found that woman and she is good to me. So, could be I don't have to be so alone. Maybe I might live as a decent man again, like when I was at sea, and right after, before they killed my wife and boy. Could be I can hang on to the woman. Then again – a man can get his head twisted with maybe and could be.'

Black Feather stood. 'That kind of talk is out there, Hawkstone. It is after and beyond. You know what we must do, now.'

'We see the old woman is comfortable first.'

'Yes.'

'I'll be headed to the banker in Tucson.'

'I will find where the regulators live and drink. We will meet at the stagecoach station north of Fort Stevens. We go to them together.'

'We can't do nothing about the cavalry. The army would swallow us up. The Wharton City marshal and his pair of cockroaches come last.'

Black Feather started for the village and the horses. He turned to look back where Hawkstone followed, the black hair sliding over his buckskin-covered shoulders. 'You got a Franklin, Hawkstone? You got a saying about them polecats?'

Hawkstone paused a few seconds in thought. '*Virtue may not always make a handsome face, but pure evil will certainly make it ugly.*'

# TWENTY-FOUR

Saguaro Claw, the old Apache woman, was dying. Burning Buffalo had her in a shallow cave high in rocks where desert bighorn sheep roamed. The day had worn itself out, and twilight offered muted trails by the time Hawkstone and

Black Feather left horses to climb among rocks and plants.

When Burning Buffalo saw them approach, he waved them to the cave. A beaded deerskin headband held his hair in place. The long pigtail hung down his back. His spear-scarred face looked sombre. They followed him on hands and knees into the cave where the old woman lay. A lantern showed the walls of the cave to be slick with wet.

The old woman's face looked placid and empty of interest or life.

Hawkstone pulled her hand out from the buffalo blanket while he watched her deep creased colourless face. She felt cold to the touch. He was aware his vision blurred, aware of the sting in his eyes and the quiver of his lower lip. Black Feather looked away, his fists clenched. She squeezed Hawkstone's hand as he bent to kiss her forehead.

In her final sigh, she whispered, 'Hattie'. And she was gone.

Behind Hawkstone, Black Feather said, 'Another life they must answer for.'

Hawkstone waited in darkness by the rock formation behind the Pima County Tucson Bank. He and Black Feather had camped beside the charred skeleton of his house. He had started before dawn for the ride to Tucson. He felt sore from his wounds and the fast full day ride, and hungry. He wanted a sip of whiskey. He was in no mood for banker nonsense. A lantern still burned inside the bank – Barron Jacobs worked late. No lights showed from the mining office fifty feet away. Jacobs had his mare tied near the back door. When the lantern blew out, Hawkstone used the banker's pony for cover. He eased the Peacemaker from its holster. Barron Jacobs wore a tan banker suit with a string tie. He wore no hat. He came out of the door, and turned to lock it.

Hawkstone grabbed a handful of his brown suit jacket collar and jammed the Colt against the back of his neck. 'You know the steps, Barron. Ease out your dainty pistol with thumb and first finger. Swing it out back here.'

Jacobs did as he was told. 'I didn't figure to see you again. I thought you'd be off spending the payroll.'

'You so sure I got it?'

'We aren't fools, Hawkstone. Apparently, you are a fool to come back here.'

'Let's hike on over to them rocks. You know the way and the place.'

Hawkstone moved the Colt back and released the banker's collar. They walked close together. Along the way Hawkstone stopped at the tied chestnut and pulled a bottle from his saddle-bag. They climbed the five feet and sat on the same boulders they had used before.

Barron Jacobs' face shone smooth and slick as the boulders. A few strands of his thick honey hair wiggled in the breeze. He looked at Hawkstone, amused. 'We've been here before. I told the marshal about you.'

'What marshal?'

'The federal marshal, Casey Steel. He's the one told me your name.'

Hawkstone kept his Colt on his leg, aimed at the banker's belly. 'Casey Steel is one of the good men. He rides an honest trail, takes pride in his work, and knows some things ain't for sale. When he gets the straight of what really happened, I reckon he won't come gunning after me.' He removed the cap from the bottle and offered it to Jacobs.

Jacobs kept his smile and shrugged and took the bottle. He gulped down a big swallow. 'How did you get all those Apache to hold up the stagecoach with you? They say there were almost forty of them.'

Hawkstone took a pull from the bottle. 'You think about

that, banker. You get an image in your head about forty Apache surrounding one stagecoach along a road through hills and rocks. You tell me how they'd all fit. They'd be strung out like a caterpillar.'

'Then who was with you?'

'Wharton City Marshal Leather Yates and his two outlaws, that's who. And they wasn't with me, they hood-winked me to go with them, after they raped and murdered my little sister. Along with shooting me, they murdered Pearl Harp just released from prison.' Hawkstone raised the Colt to tap it against Jacob's forehead. 'You quit jawing about the stagecoach. You know nothing was on it.'

Barron Jacobs leaned away from the tapping weapon. 'I know you hit our pony riders and took the saddle-bags. They said they thought you had three Apache with you.'

'That is correct, banker.'

'Then you have the money.'

'I know where it is – less the ten per cent reward fee.'

Jacobs shook his handsome head, loosening a few more honey strands. 'No, that isn't how it works. You turn in *all* the money, *then* we give you the ten per cent, maybe.'

Hawkstone gave the bottle to the banker. 'You got any kinda image of that happening? I don't trust you no more than I trust city marshals. I'll tell you where the money is. You tell Casey Steel. They got to dig it up from a grave on the west side of some pines next to my burned-up house. Steel and his men will find a coupla bodies down there, shot down by the owner of the boots, which they will also find.'

'Then he can arrest him.'

'Ain't nothing in the coming days got anything to do with arrest.'

'Should I also tell Steel about what you did to those people in the stagecoach?'

'I was one of them people. I got shot down, just like them folks did. I can show you the bullet holes, but I ain't got the time.'

'Steel will come after you. He'll get a posse and hunt you down.'

'Mebbe not when he finds out who the real shooters – about to be deceased – were.'

'You mean this fellow, Yates?'

'And his scum shadow shooters, One Eye Tim Brace and Wild Fletch Badger – which brings me to another item we got to discuss. Tell me about them gunmen regulators. Who pays them?'

Jacobs slugged down another swallow. 'They guard the payroll shipments and patrol the copper mines.'

'Now, Barron, that ain't what I asked you. Who pays them?'

'Longfellow Copper Mining.'

'The mines paid them to massacre Apache in a small village?'

'Just like the savages did to those in the stagecoach.'

Hawkstone sighed deep, jerking when he felt pain. 'None of you jaspers get it. There weren't no Apache. The village they destroyed was innocent. Them blue belly soldiers and the regulator gunmen, and the marshal and his pair killed and looted for no reason.'

'So you say. They scalped the Longfellow vice-president. And who are you? A thief and a killer yourself. You were sent to prison for robbing a bank. You even killed a teller. I don't believe you any more than you trust me.'

'I was the only survivor of the stagecoach slaughter – me and them that did the killing. And it weren't Apache. They faked it to look that way. Not one was from that village.'

Hawkstone drained the last of the whiskey from the bottle. He held it in his hand with the Colt on his leg again and stared at Jacobs' knee.

Barron Jacobs squinted at him. 'You trying to decide whether to shoot me or not?'

'Yup. Will you tell Casey Steel what I said?'

'I'm not sure.'

'You'll get your money back, eventually, unless you're in a hurry and go on out there with some boys and dig it up yourself.'

'Not *all* the money, Hawkstone.' He rubbed his chin. 'Yes, all right. I'll tell him. But I'm riding out there with him to see if what you're saying is true. If it is, there will be arrests.'

'I already told you, banker,' Hawkstone said, 'and you can tell this to the marshal. There ain't gonna be no arrests.'

# TWENTY-FIVE

Saturday night, ten miles before Fort Webster, Hawkstone heard the whoop and holler of gathered men a quarter mile before he reached the horse change way station. When he left the bank, he slept four hours by the Rio Gila, and thought about riding the trail out of his way towards Fort McLane, to Rachel Good Squaw, the medicine woman. But that would take too long, and Black Feather waited.

At least twenty horses were tethered outside the one big room with attached living quarters; so many that the rail couldn't hold them, so a rope string tie stretched from the rail to the corral fence. Two wagons sat across the road.

Inside, blue uniforms dominated windows and the open door as young soldiers worked to out-shout each other. Four youthful women with experience beyond their years drank 'corn liquor' and laughed hollow and allowed themselves to get pawed. Hawkstone knew Black Feather would not be allowed inside. He'd be looking for the chestnut, knowing it was a two-day ride from Tucson. Beyond the strung horses and room noise, Black Feather stepped out on to the road and waved a hand. Hawkstone rode over and tied his chestnut to the corral fence next to the appaloosa stallion.

Together off their mounts, they watched a young pony soldier stagger out the door and vomit on his boots. They moved behind the end horse on the string.

'They are bunched together,' Black Feather said.

'Who?'

'This is where the regulators come to eat and drink. The three are in there now.'

In lantern light from the door and windows, Hawkstone pulled his Colt. He slid a cartridge into the chamber kept empty for the hammer to rest when moving about. The Peacemaker was so sensitive a bump or fall or fist fight might have the hammer send a bullet into a man's leg or foot. Now, he needed all six – twelve shots with Black Feather's Colt. The Winchester was too cumbersome for close quarters. He rotated the cylinder to make sure he had a full load. 'We can't take them inside.'

'They drink apart from the blue bellies. They are not alone.'

Hawkstone frowned. 'What do you mean?'

'The five murdering soldiers drink with them.'

'How do you know?'

'I watch them through the window. They are drunk and they brag. They show silver and gold they found in the village. It is as if they are an exclusive club, as if they share what they did with pride.'

Hawkstone saw the fire in Black Feather's dark eyes, and stepped out from the end horse to the road. The soldier with vomit on his boots went back inside. Hawkstone looked hard at his blood brother. 'I want them dead. I don't want to know what they look like, or how they dress, or what spawned them, or what future they look to, or their plans or dreams or who or what they love. They got to die for what they done to our village. How do we get them out here?'

'With bait.'

Hawkstone nodded. 'The girl, Charlotte. The family lives in the back. There's got to be another entrance. Cauley and Rose-Marie work the counter. The girl must be in there with the soldiers.'

'You talk to the boy.'

'Sled.'

Hawkstone moved away from the front of the building and went round the back. There was a porch with a roof at the back door. Sled, in pants only with bare feet, sat on a porch step smoking a rolled Bull Durham cigarette.

Sled looked up at Hawkstone and started to flip the cigarette, then stopped and nodded. 'I know you. You come to visit a while back. You helped me with the team.'

'The name is Hawkstone.'

'You was with the Apache.'

'He's waiting by the horses.' Hawkstone sat next to Sled on the step. He pulled the makings for his own smoke. 'Sled, I got an ugly story to tell you about some men inside. I want you and Charlotte to help us out. You each got a five dollar gold piece if you do.'

Sled ran fingers through his tousled brown hair. 'Who we got to shoot?'

'Not shoot, bait. Me and my blood brother will do the shooting.'

Hawkstone told Sled about the village slaughter and plunder, told who did it, and where they now stood, laughing and showing trinkets and slapping each other with guffaws of pride in victory over savages who no longer belonged and had to be exterminated. The whole time Hawkstone talked, Sled nodded and smoked.

Leaving Sled, Hawkstone went unnoticed through the front door and among them. The room smelled like lilac, as sickly perfumed as a funeral parlor. Some soldiers didn't bathe or splash on lilac water, and offered a different scent. A girl stumbled into his arms spreading her honeysuckle aroma and blinked with little success to get his face in focus. She was coming out of the top of her velvet red dress and a scar creased the side of her neck. She had squinty brown eyes and needed much paint to look pretty. She asked if she knew him, then stumbled away without an answer. He pushed through uniforms towards the counter where the eight men stood in a tight circle. Cauley broke past him without recognition, his face drawn with worry as he carried bottles of 'corn liquor' and glasses on a tray. The ma, Rose-Marie, stood behind the counter with her raw red hands clutching her neck to frame her drawn face. Her nervous eyes darted around the room, as if she felt surrounded by hostility.

Four of the eight men leaned back against the counter, faces flushed with drink, and friendly. The three civilian-dressed regulators wore their guns handy, one low, two high on their hip, all tied tight. Their friendly looks appeared false and did not show in their eyes. They studied the room, where each soldier stood, where the girls were. The five soldiers stood close on both sides of the regulators, their young eyes staring at soiled doves with hunger. All of them watched the fourteen year-old girl approach in her short pink calico dress.

One regulator leaned low to the girl cupping his ear with his hand. 'Happy to meet you, Charlotte, I'm Whit. Show us what, sweetie?'

The girl stood on tip-toes to talk again in his ear. His palm rested flat on her back. The other men kept their eyes on her.

'Out the back?' Whit asked. 'You want us to follow you? All of us?' He stood straight. 'Honey, you can't be that experienced.'

'No, no,' she said. 'It ain't like that. Well, not exactly. I wanna know who kisses best.'

A dark-skinned soldier pushed between the girl and Whit. 'Hey, fellas, she's only fourteen.'

'She sure don't look like no fourteen,' Whit said. He leaned toward the girl again. 'Sweetie, we can take care of any kissin' business right here. No need to go outside.' He moved his hand down her back.

Charlotte ducked away. 'Too noisy,' the girl said, 'my ma and pa can see. Come on.' She moved around the counter and danced towards a kitchen, bedroom and the back door.

The eight men looked at each other, shrugged, and followed Charlotte.

Hawkstone walked five steps behind them, the rawhide loop off his Colt. He watched their backs. The regulators looked in their early thirties. Not one of the soldiers appeared past twenty-five. As his breath quickened, Hawkstone eased out the Colt and had to ask himself, why? What would possess young army men to ride through a small village shooting children and women, and then steal whatever they might find? Did the mind behind their white skin hate the Apache that much? Or did they listen to tall tales by old sergeants about the evils of the heathen? None of it mattered now. The men were little more than moving targets. The soldiers had flaps on their holsters which would slow their draw. The regulators had to go first.

When they reached the back porch, Sled waited. 'This is the way, boys.'

Sled and Charlotte took off at a run towards the string of horses, each five dollars richer. They ducked under the string and disappeared.

Black Feather stood in front of the men with his Colt in his hand. 'You murdered and looted my little village,' he said.

'Fill your hands, buzzards,' Hawkstone said coming down the steps and moving to the right.

Whit grabbed his pistol. 'It looks like we ain't done with killing.'

Black Feather shot him through the head.

'Over here, sheep dips,' Hawkstone said.

All pistols came out. Hawkstone shot one, then another. They twisted and fell. Two of the three regulators died quick and first. Black Feather made each of two shots count. The snap of pistol fire caused horses to jump and yank against the string line until it broke. Dirt and dust from shuffling boots and falling men, and white gunsmoke clouded the back of the station as horses panicked and ran off down the road past the entrance. Men inside the building shuffled and shouted and demanded to know what was going on.

One soldier stared, his face wrinkled in tears, his eyes not believing, fiddling with the flap, his gun still in his holster. The third regulator next to him aimed at Hawkstone.

The soldier boy fumbled with his pistol and tried to get it clear.

'Pull it out, son,' Hawkstone said. 'You got to pay like the others.'

141

Black Feather shot the boy through the back of his head. Hawkstone ducked as two bullets zinged and slipped past close to his temple. He returned fire and the regulator and two more soldiers stumbled and fell. Surprise and drunkenness kept them from being sharp, kept them from staying alive. Pistols dropped from their hands. Hawkstone fired against anyone on the ground moving. He kept at it until all six cartridges sent bullets into a body or head. Twenty seconds had passed. He was ready to reload but all three regulators and five young cavalry soldiers lay dead in the dirt.

Feet stomped as men came running out the front door. By then, Black Feather had already reached his appaloosa and swung his leg on up. Hawkstone had the chestnut running as he jumped into the saddle, ignoring pain from his healing wounds. They galloped as fast as their mounts could run away from the front of the building, riding hard towards the hills, towards the copper mines. Hawkstone saw Black Feather up ahead sway as the appaloosa pounded the dirt road in a fast run, and knew his blood brother had been hit.

# TWENTY-SIX

Wharton City Marshal Leather Yates sat in his office chair listening to the groans and cries from the Apache they had found. The marshal's desk was cluttered with old 'Wanted' posters and messages and filled-out complaint forms – work he had been too busy to address, what with holding up stagecoaches and lighting fires and shooting male and female culprits and raiding hostile villages and such. Since One Eye Tim Brace and Wild Fletch Badger were recognized deputies now – and too proud of their badges – the marshal didn't have to ride to the Way Out Saloon for whispered meetings: they met locally at Slim's Saloon, which carried higher class and even had three friendly upstairs women, or they met in the marshal's office. The office, a lean-to connected to the much larger Gentlemen Kingdom building, run by Vicki Verona, stood about twenty-five feet wall to wall with the desk and chair, three wooden armed guest chairs and a locked cabinet holding old rim-fire rifles and a double-barrel twelve gauge. All windows had bars. Down a sixteen-foot hallway were the two eight-foot barred cells, with the Apache in one of them, getting worked over by One Eye Tim Brace and Wild Fletch Badger.

Wild Fletch came into the office from the cell rubbing the buckskin leather glove-covered knuckles of his right fist. His cheek puffed with a wad of tobacco. He turned his head to spit.

'Use the spittoon,' Yates said.

Fletch tried but missed. 'The neck is too small. You need a bucket.'

'You spit all over my cell block floor?'

'Not too much. We got his name. He's called Burning Buffalo. When we hauled him from the funeral fire, I reckon the old woman burning was like the matriarch, like the leader of the village that once was. Mebbe this Burning Buffalo was the last of the village hostiles.'

'No. The late Anson Hawkstone's young sidekick, Black Feather, is lurking about someplace. Mebbe gettin' ready to dig up that payroll cash, plus the ten thousand from the Mineral City bank job three years ago. We got to deal with him soon.' The marshal sat stiff. 'Uh oh.'

They watched through the barred window as a man with a handlebar mustache stomped with purpose to the door and came in. He stood in front of the desk, his flat round face shining bright red with anger under the black bowler hat.

'Marshal!' he said. 'If you don't do somethin', I'm gonna shoot somebody dead.'

The marshal held up his chubby hands. 'Now, Piver, ain't no use gettin' in a tizzy fit.'

'You got my complaint there in that pile on your desk. I tell you his fence is two feet across my property. I told him and told him but he don't pay no attention.'

'Got it right here, Piver.' Yates slid papers around and glanced at Wild Fetch, who stood quiet. The marshal gave up looking. 'I'll get right on it.'

Piver glanced at Wild Fletch. He squinted when a groan came from the cell out behind the office. He looked back at the marshal. 'You been away so much, some of us wonder why we re-elected you. How come you don't stay in town and mind the business here?'

Yates pushed his bulk back out of the chair. He waddled around the desk and patted Piver on the shoulder. 'I will. I had out-of-town business to tend to, but from now on what happens in Wharton City will be my top concern. You get what I'm saying, Piver? You understand?'

Piver sighed. 'Well, that fence has got to go. When you gonna tell him?'

'Today, or first thing tomorrow morning.' Yates put his arm around Piver's shoulders and eased him to the door. 'Now, you go on over to Slim's and get yourself a good stiff drink, on me – how is Amy, that sweet darlin' wife of yours?'

'Just as upset about that fence as me. Marshal, you got to. . . .'

'I know, I know, and I will.' Yates got Piver out the door

and headed for Slim's Saloon.

Wild Fletch said, 'Want me to look into it, Marshal?'

Marshal Leather Yates jerked straight and leaned back against the door, his brow wrinkled in surprise. 'You?'

'I'm a deputy. It's part of my job.'

'You, a deputy? You ain't that kind of deputy. You're a hired killer deputy, and don't you forget it.'

Wild Fletch tapped his badge. 'This here says I'm a regular lawman. I can do all the normal stuff a lawman does. I can. I want to prove it.'

The marshal returned to stand by his desk. 'Just prove you ain't as stupid as your sidekick in there. Come on. Let's hope One Eye hasn't killed the savage yet.'

Back by the cell, Yates saw the savage in a heap on the cell floor. Burning Buffalo had a lot of blood around him. One Eye stood tall and turned to them, breathing hard, his gloved fists doubled, stained with blood. His hat was on the cot and he looked like a one-eyed scarecrow.

Wild Fletch said, 'What you find out?'

The one eye blinked as his breathing slowed. 'I don't answer to you, dung spitter.' He jabbed his tin star with his thumb. 'I'm a deputy jest like you.'

Wild Fletch bit a plug of tobacco. 'I got seniority. I got made deputy afore you.'

The marshal said, 'Don't be slippin' off the rails, boys. The payroll – we got to think about the payroll we *didn't* find on the stagecoach.' He nodded to the Apache on the floor. 'What'd he tell you?'

One Eye stared at Wild Fletch as if waiting for the first spit. 'I got equal seniority. Marshal, you tell him we're the same level of deputy.'

Marshal Leather Yates sighed exasperated. 'I'll yank them badges from the pair of you and shove 'em where no light ever reaches. You fellas got to be thinkin' what's important – and it ain't tin stars shinin' on your vest. Do we know where Black Feather's tepee used to stand?'

'Not yet,' One Eye said. 'He's an Injun, he ain't saying a hell of a lot.'

Yates looked from one to the other, then at the lump on the cell floor. 'The money is buried someplace in that village. I figure somebody got the shot-up village bodies buried by now, or they're at it. We got to take shovels out there, and you deputies start digging. It's either under where Black Feather's tepee stood, or someplace next to the old woman's wickiup. Bring good shovels 'cause you got some holes to dig. We'll find it, boys, I know we will. We deserve it.'

One Eye kicked the curled bulk of Burning Buffalo. 'I'll get him to talk. He knows where the cash is.'

'I need some coffee,' the marshal said, 'laced with good spirit.' He waddled down the hall back to his desk chair, and poured coffee and whiskey in a cup half-and-half. With a grimace he rubbed the back of his leg at the dog bite – it stiffened his leg on occasion, the way a cramp had a man pounding his foot and rubbing to get rid of it. He sat, while the noise of the beating continued in the cell. He rifled through papers looking for Piver's complaint, then gave up and tossed the papers aside.

When the second cup of coffee was about done, the marshal nodded, eyelids heavy, his pudgy hands resting on his ample belly, his pork-chop whiskers bobbing with his head, a snore coming out. He no longer listened to the beating. He dreamed of young girls at Gentlemen Kingdom next door, of him having the youngest just starting out. He remembered the young girl by the river, Hattie Smooth Water. She'd been brand new and he'd been first. He'd carry the fond memory for the rest of his life. He'd never been first before with anyone. He relived each moment with her, smiling because of the details. His teeth clamped tight when he caught the vision of what Wild Fletch Badger did to her. The gunslinger should have died for that. Not too late. He saw a future minus his two deputies. Someday. Soon. When they found the money.

One Eye Tim Brace came down the hallway from the cell. He bounced from wall to wall as if he was drunk. A gag came out of him as if he was about to vomit. He stumbled into the office, bumped into the side of the desk and fell, more than sat, in an office chair. 'Christ,' he said. His face was white as sheep wool. The one eye stared big as a quarter. 'The Injun went and died on us.' The cavity looked like the inside of a small ashtray, always carrying dirt and dust and debris of one kind or another.

Yates found One Eye Tim Brace about as grotesque and ugly as a man could be. He looked a little better with his hat. Why didn't he go get his hat? Why didn't he wear an eye patch over the cavity or get one of them marble false eyeballs like others who lost an eye? One Eye once told Yates he liked the mean image, made him look scary to people he wanted to frighten. The marshal sat straight with a frown. 'What's that? He's gone? Did he tell you where the tepee was?'

'Yeah.' One Eye's voice sounded strained. 'Third site in from the northeast corner.'

'That ain't all he told you, is it Tim?'

'That one in there and three others held up a Pony Express string and got the payroll. They got the cash buried all right.'

'Did he say where?'

'No. Except he said it mighta been by the burned shack, 'cept he didn't know for sure.'

'True or not, we can at least go for the ten thousand. What else? That wasn't all.'

'No sir, no sir, that ain't all.' He rubbed his hand across his lips.

'What is it?'

One Eye Tim Brace leaned forward, ugly and sweating. 'Before he went gone, he told me, Anson Hawkstone ain't dead.'

# TWENTY-SEVEN

Just at dawn, Hawkstone felt the soft warmth of the medicine woman push against him. Her long red hair covered his face. He took his sweet time exploring her with his palms. He wasn't sure when Black Feather left his blankets to wander the village. He seldom heard the movement out of the hut. He did know the girl Little Rain followed Black Feather like an obedient puppy, though not ten words had passed between them.

Rachel's lips touched his ear. 'Are you strong enough for this?'

'No, but it don't matter.'

'I already had to restitch and burn that shoulder. I don't want to do it again.'

'It might be worth it. *When the well is dry, we know the wealth of water.*'

Rachel chuckled. 'Another Franklin? You ain't been dry since you got here.'

'You see to that.'

'And I'm about to again.'

Mid-morning, Hawkstone had the chestnut in the river. Without boots, he stood in water to his calves, washing the mare's back and neck and scooping water on her. He rubbed her with an old piece of calico and her shoulders shivered while her head moved up and down as if pleased. He talked low to her, telling her what a fine mount she was.

Black Feather led his appaloosa to the water and began to splash water over the stallion's back. 'When?' he said.

'It's more'n a two-day ride. You think the prisoner wagons been there yet? Yates will be watching that.'

'Maybe he go to burned house, find grave, get payroll money.'

'I figure Casey Steel will get there first, then come looking for Yates. How's your side?'

'I can ride. We both too shot up for racing horses. We maybe take two and a half days.'

'My trigger finger works jest fine. We gotta make sure they're still there.'

'They will search until they find something.'

'Where did you keep the Mineral City money?'

'Wrapped in a buffalo hide, against a tepee wall. Now your woman has it.'

Hawkstone wrung the calico and wiped down the filly. 'How old is that girl follows you around?'

'She is eighteen. She tells me she will always follow.'

Hawkstone squinted at Black Feather. 'Will she?'

'Perhaps. She is easy to look at and she is good to fix the side wound. She likes to help the medicine woman heal others. She has a good heart and carries more smiles than frowns. But she may be too gentle.'

'Ain't no such thing as a woman too gentle.'

'We will see what happens. When do we go?'

'I reckon about noon,' Hawkstone said.

On the second day of riding, in a twilight that pushed down the sun and cloaked the land grey, Hawkstone and Black Feather crossed the Rio Gila river and walked their ponies towards Disappointment Creek. Before they reached what had been the village, they aimed their mounts to the hills on their right, beyond the other end of the site. They moved in shadows now, for night had almost come. Hawkstone did not want to climb as high as the cliff-dwelling rock-desert sheep and goats, just high enough to see the village site clear before it all became black. They found a flat ledge large enough for them and the horses, and stopped and dismounted and looked down at the clearing that had once been a tribal village. They remained silent. Hawkstone did not know what thoughts went through his blood brother's thinking. His own pondering was a mix of grief and anger. He still felt the flutter in his chest, the finger flexing of his healing gun hand. The soldier boys and gunman regulators who took part were dead. This was the finish of it, the killing dead end of it.

The village bodies had been taken by Federal Marshal Casey Steel and his two wagons of Yuma Territorial convicts and buried somewhere Hawkstone did not want to know. It must have been a grisly business. Vultures took care of left-over titbits of flesh. Ashes and rubble still marked the locations of tepees and wickiups. Toward the end of the clearing, closest to the creek, Hawkstone saw the skeletal remains of the old woman's wickiup. No more was visible in the darkness.

Hawkstone and Black Feather kept their mounts saddled. They built no campfire but ate cold antelope jerky and drank water. After eating, they sat with their backs against a rock wall and lit smokes and passed a whiskey bottle.

'They will not come at night,' Black Feather said, 'unless they know we wait and want to ambush us. They will come with the sun.'

Hawkstone drew in a drag from the cigarette. 'Before they die they must feel the loss of their private parts. They must know the pain because of Hattie.'

'Yes. We will shoot them slow, a little at a time.'

They sat and looked down on the clearing and passed the bottle. Hawkstone spoke part of his thinking. 'For Hattie – for what they done to Hattie. They ain't men, nobody can say such. They're something less, less than human. I knew plenty like them when I scouted for the army up around Santa Fe. It was how they acted towards tribes. Mebbe when men get shed of home and hearth, leaving a loving woman where they walk tall in the eyes of their young 'uns, they throw out everything they left behind, scrape off any civilized thinking. They see them as savages, as cur, and don't see nothing to justify them living and having a life like them. They want the children killed so no more generations come along.'

Black Feather said, 'You got too much Apache thinking in you.'

'Mebbe not enough.'

They sat silent until the bottle was empty. Black Feather moved away far enough to pee. He came back and grimaced as he sat from the pain in his side. 'When we arc done, I will not return to the hut of your woman or her village.'

Hawkstone stared at him. 'What about the girl, Little Rain?'

'She will live a happy life without me.'

'Collect her and take her with you.'

151

'When we are done, I will want to be alone. I will ride to Mexico, and when I am ready, I will find people of my own kind and mingle with them. You are my blood brother, but I have no more patience with the white man. He irritates me when he comes among us. I don't like him coupled with our women. I don't like our women to lay with him.'

Hawkstone sat with his knees up, staring down at the darkness below. He turned to Black Feather. 'Tell me where you'll be.'

Black Feather sighed. 'I cannot tell you because I do not know. I only tell you that when we are done, I will ride away.'

Hawkstone nodded. 'I reckon you know best.'

'And what of you, Hawkstone? You will return to the medicine woman?'

'For as long as I can. They may come after me, and I'll have to ride out.'

'To where?'

'Mebbe to Montana or Wyoming Territory. I'd want Rachel to come with me, but she won't. She figures I'd always come back to her, and she ain't gonna give up what she has.' He shrugged. 'Who knows? When the dust settles I might jest drift back this way.'

Black Feather nodded. He stretched. 'Now, you send us to sleep with a Franklin, my brother.'

Hawkstone leaned back. '*Evil must cloak itself. Truth can go naked.*'

# TWENTY-EIGHT

They came at late morning the next day, as Hawkstone and Black Feather watched, watched not from the exposed ledge, but behind ground-level rocks large enough to hide the horses. Sunlight brought out a lingering death smell from the earth. Crows had returned to the cottonwoods, flying down on occasion to snap up spotted rotten flesh. The three rode in, walking their mounts, weapons in their hands. The rotund Wharton City marshal led them down the length of the butchery site, then back. At the ash rubble that had been Black Feather's tepee, the marshal holstered his Colt and watched the other two do the same.

'All right, gents,' he said. 'Think like an Apache. You got this cash, this money another fella stole, and you're gonna hide it for him. Do you step off ten paces or fifty paces and claw at the dirt?' He scanned the horizon around him.

'No,' Wild Fletch said. He swung down and pulled the shovel tied to his saddle and spat a gob of tobacco juice. 'That's the white man way. If I'm Apache I bury it inside the tepee, in the centre where I sleep and eat and drink, and fool around with Apache women.'

'Yeah,' One Eye said. He swung down and pulled his shovel. 'Let's start digging.'

The two men stood in the centre of the circled rubble and began to dig standing opposite each other. The marshal Yates grunted as he swung down from his animal. At the saddle-bag, he pulled a small bottle of whiskey. He rubbed the back of his leg and stood uneasy, as if he was not used to standing. He said, 'Did you boys bury the redskin where I told you?'

One Eye paused, breathing heavy. 'Burning Buffalo, yeah, an hour from the Way Out Saloon, to the west like you said.'

'Good. I told you Hawkstone made me walk naked from there back to the saloon. It's good his friend is buried there, after my deputies beat him to death.'

Protected by chest-high rocks, looking at the digging, Hawkstone saw Black Feather's face muscles tighten. Black Feather reached for his Colt, but did not pull it. Instead, he grabbed Hawkstone's arm and nodded to the southwest at a dirt cloud. Riders were coming from where the burned house sat.

Mesquite and dry grass and sage spread beyond the village site. The land spread flat to shallow hills and showed three riders coming, and the marshal had not seen them yet. Behind them, rocky hills rose to mesas towards the Rio Gila.

Hawkstone and Black Feather stared at each other. Hawkstone was undecided. Hit the three now, or wait for what was coming? They waited, while the two deputies dug, their deputy badges shining in the sunlight.

As the three riders rode closer, Hawkstone recognized Federal Marshal Casey Steel in the lead by his black Montana Peak Stetson. They rode at a fast trot, the two with him wearing deputy badges. They were almost at the village when Yates saw them.

One Eye looked up from his digging. 'What is it, Marshal?'

Yates stared at the coming riders. 'Better ease up on the diggin', boys. Get rid of them shovels.'

They tossed the shovels towards a mesquite bush and

stood by the hole watching with the marshal. The marshal fixed his pork-chop whiskered face with a polite grin as the three federal men rode up.

Casey Steel touched the brim of his Stetson. 'Leather?'

'Casey?' Leather Yates said. 'You're a long way from Tucson.'

Steel sat on his mount without moving. The two deputies split apart on each side of him. The horses with empty saddles moved away. Steel said, 'On the right there is Burt White, left is Jess Cassidy. We been digging out at the burned Hawkstone place.' He nodded at the hole. 'I see you boys been shovelling some on your own.'

'That's jest fascinatin', Casey,' Yates said. 'You find anything interesting?'

Burt White, with a full black beard and a bowler hat, said, 'What are you digging for?'

Yates ignored him. 'What brings you here, Casey?'

'An arrest warrant.'

'What's that?' Yates said, his hand going easy to his holster.

To Casey's left, Jess Cassidy with a deep creased bare face and grey plains hat, pulled from his holster and said, 'Don't think about doing that.'

Casey Steel stepped down from his horse and drew his Colt. 'You're under arrest, Leather Yates, for the murder of Big Ears Kate and Billy Bob Crutch. I found their grave, along with your boots.'

'My *boots*?'

'Buried along with forty-three thousand and two hundred in cash – which the banker fella with us took back to Tucson. Seems it was supposed to be forty-eight thousand, but somebody skimmed it.'

Leather Yates breathed heavy through his nose. 'Anson Hawkstone. He buried my boots with the cash and Big Ears

155

Kate and Billy Bob on account of he stole the money and skimmed it and killed them two.'

'That's a lie,' Hawkstone said as he and Black Feather came out from the rocks.

The men stared at the two, coming at them with Colts in their hands, their horses still hidden.

Yates returned his attention to Casey Steel. 'You can't arrest me, you ain't got the authority.'

'I'm a Federal Marshal, Yates. I represent the United States Government. And we ain't even mentioned the butchery that went on here. You was part of that.'

'It was all legal, with the United States Army leading it. You ain't gonna hold me for that. I'm a city marshal – I was elected by town citizens – elected. Some politician appointed you. You ain't gonna arrest me, Steel. Not on account of my boots,' he pointed to Hawkstone, 'that he planted to make me look guilty.'

Casey Steel glanced up at his deputies. They both swung down from their saddles, weapons in their hands. One pulled out handcuffs. Steel said, 'That's what the warrant is about, but that ain't why I'm arresting you. You and your two cockroaches raped and murdered an Apache girl down by the Rio Bravo. A boy saw you and run to his pa. They pulled the girl from the river. I'm gonna see all three of you hung for that.'

One Eye said, 'She was jest some Apache. We was funnin' with her. Nobody gonna hang us for some Apache.'

The men stood about eight feet apart in a semi-circle, their horses behind them. Hawkstone watched Wild Fletch Badger's right hand down by the holster, fingers quivering.

'You'll hang for sure,' Casey Steel said.

The quickest draw of them all was gunfighter Wild Fletch Badger. He spat out a gob of tobacco juice and before anyone could move, drew and shot Federal Marshal Casey

156

Steel in the chest. Steel stumbled back. Horses jerked back and moved away. Hawkstone shot Fletch Badger in the gun wrist, cocked and shot Leather Yates in the leg. Badger dropped his gun and grabbed his wrist. He crouched, released the wrist, and his left hand groped in the dirt for the gun. Yates twisted down to his fat knee. The snap of gunshots echoed across the hollow empty village site and out across the barren land.

Black Feather shot One Eye through his vacant socket and again quickly through the throat, then took a step forward and shot him twice below his belly button. While Casey Steel fell, Yates shot Deputy Burt White through his black beard. The other deputy, Jess Cassidy, shot Yates in the back. Fletch Badger had his pistol in his left hand. He fired and hit Cassidy in the shoulder. Black Feather aimed low and shot Leather Yates below his ample stomach straight through the crotch, fired again higher, into the stomach. Yates doubled and fell back.

Hawkstone stepped close enough to push his Colt against Wild Fletch Badger's stomach, aimed a little lower to the crotch and fired twice. Badger screamed as Hawkstone stepped back and shot him through the heart.

After white gunsmoke curled away in the breeze and the ear-pounding shooting had stopped, three men remained on their feet – Hawkstone, Black Feather, and the Federal Deputy Jess Cassidy. Hawkstone and Black Feather kept their aim at the deputy. The man stood like stone, sharp face clean and creased, left hand against his shoulder, his Colt aimed at Hawkstone.

'We're done,' Hawkstone said. 'It's up to you.'

Marshal Casey Steel moved and groaned.

Cassidy holstered his Colt and went to the marshal and kneeled beside him. 'We'll get you help.'

Casey Steel blinked and looked beyond the deputy to

Hawkstone. He lay back with his eyes closed.

Hawkstone said, 'We'll get him on his horse.'

'All of them,' Cassidy said. 'I'll string the bodies to Wharton City, get a wagon and after a doc sees him, take the marshal back to Tucson.' He stood straight and looked from Black Feather to Hawkstone. 'What about you two?'

'We're done with all of this.'

'You better come to Tucson and clear it up.'

'I don't see that happening, deputy. We'll be gone.'

Cassidy stood silent for a spell, his flinty grey-eyed stare going from one to the other. He nodded, and turned his attention to the marshal.

The three of them draped the bodies over mounts and tied them down. Casey Steel sat hunched over his horse. Deputy Jess Cassidy led the rope-connected horses out of the village site and towards the Rio Gila river.

Black Feather reloaded his Colt. While Hawkstone watched the string of bodies move out of sight, he fetched the horses and led them down to his tepee site. He swung his leg over the appaloosa. He smiled at Hawkstone. 'Until next time my blood brother. You got a Franklin to leave me by?'

Hawkstone said, '*Enjoy the present, remember the past, but neither fear nor wish the appearance of the last.*'

Black Feather rode south, and Anson Hawkstone watched until he was out of sight. He reloaded his Colt and with it back in the holster, mounted the chestnut, mindful of his wounds. He wriggled to sit well in the saddle. His gaze went the length of the village and came to rest at what used to be the old woman's wickiup. He had known comfort and happiness in the village, and carried fondness for the people living there. As some parts of a life went, the village now spread cold and dead. Gently, he heeled the chestnut and reined her to ride easy for the Rio Gila. After crossing the river, he'd start his two-day journey to the village where Rachel Cleary, now Rachel Good Squaw, the medicine woman, waited for him.